Carrie Nichols grew up in New England, but moved south and traded snow for central AC. She loves to travel, is addicted to British crime dramas and knows a *Seinfeld* quote appropriate for every occasion.

A 2016 RWA Golden Heart® winner and two-time Maggie Award for Excellence winner, she has one tolerant husband, two grown sons and two critical cats. To her dismay, Carrie's characters—like her family—often ignore the wisdom and guidance she offers.

D0756068

THE MARINE'S SECRET DAUGHTER

CARRIE NICHOLS

MILLS & BOON

First Published in Great Britain 2018
by Mills & Boon, an imprint of HarperCollins*Publishers*
1 London Bridge Street, London, SE1 9GF

The Marine's Secret Daughter © 2018 Carol Opalinski

ISBN: 978-0-263-26473-9

38-0218

MIX
Paper from
responsible sources
FSC™ C007454

This book is produced from independently certified FSC™ paper to ensure responsible forest management.

For more information visit: www.harpercollins.co.uk/green

Printed and bound in Spain
by CPI, Barcelona

This is for my very own heroes,
John, Alex and Michael, and for the heroines
who love them, Jess and Caitlin.

Chapter One

The truth could be inconvenient, but he'd be damned if he'd give those doctors the satisfaction of being right.

Riley Cooper slammed the door of his truck and rolled his shoulder to work out the stiffness, but all that time on the road without anything stronger than ibuprofen hadn't helped. The doc had prescribed Percocet, but the meds made him drowsy. And the way he figured it, taking the drugs would be an easy out, considering the pain his buddies had died with, and their families still lived with. At the base hospital, they'd prodded and poked him and labeled his condition survivor's guilt. The way they'd said *condition* had him grinding his molars. They wanted guilt? Being tucked away in the tranquil mountains of Vermont instead of Afghanistan, leading his men—now *that* was guilt.

The therapist had told him, *You need to take time to*

*heal your body and clear your head before I can sign
off on your return to combat. Take thirty days, Sergeant,
and maybe I'll consider putting you back in theater.*

Riley's fist tightened around the key as the therapist's
words swirled in his head like debris kicked up from he-
licopter rotor wash. His shoulder was healing, and except for the occasional ringing in his ears, he was good.
Damn good. He needed to get back to Afghanistan, to
his men, to his life, not spend time in the back of beyond,
losing his edge. He wasn't himself here in this peaceful
town, but on the battlefield, he had a purpose, a reason
to do what he was doing and men to protect.

Vegas for R&R had been an option, but summers
spent at Loon Lake with the McBrides were treasured
memories from his childhood. Warm days spent with
Liam exploring the woods, building forts, swimming.
All with Liam's younger sister, Meggie, trailing behind.
Coming to the lake wouldn't bring those days back, but
this place might provide some measure of comfort.

The two cottages were one hundred yards from the
main road and surrounded on three sides by trees, making it seem as if they were the only buildings in the
wilderness. A shared driveway meant one entrance for
vehicles, easy to guard and—

Chill, Marine, you're not on duty.

He stood in the driveway of his rented cottage and
stared next door. With its open porch and natural clapboard siding, the neighboring cottage mirrored this one
except for its state of disrepair, which confirmed what
he'd heard. The McBrides had not used the cottage after
Mrs. McBride's death. But as far as he knew, widower
Mac still owned the place, unlike Riley's parents, who'd
sold theirs during the divorce because each couldn't

stand the thought of the other one having it. The way he figured it, the cottage came out ahead.

Two bright red Adirondack chairs on the porch across the yard caught his attention. *Strange.* Those chairs appeared freshly painted. He scanned the area, searching for other anomalies. An engine noise sent him into a crouch until he realized it was an outboard motor; not surprising since the lake was beyond the trees.

Stand down, Marine, there are no armed insurgents in Loon Lake.

He cursed under his breath. Even here, in this placid setting, the vigilance remained. He still felt the initial numbness from the blast wave, the acrid cordite stinging his nose, Private Trejo's screams filling his ears.

He took a deep breath and held it before releasing. No smoke. No burning flesh. Just clean air and evergreens. Situation normal.

Last time he'd been here, his head had been filled with Meghan McBride, not hostiles. But that was before, and if nothing else, Afghanistan had shown him what he was capable of. He'd seen too much, done too much, and would never be the man Meggie had once loved. He sighed and stretched his neck.

He turned his back on the McBrides' vacation home, shoved those thoughts into a box marked "regrets" and locked it tight. A bit of time to heal and he'd be on his way…back to where life had a purpose. When he was in a mine-resistant armored carrier, scouting routes for vehicle convoys or picking spots for marine units to bivouac overnight in the field, thinking about Meggie had kept him company and provided a sweet torture. Three years after enlisting and leaving Meggie behind, he'd returned for his Gran's funeral and discovered the

skinny girl he'd spent summers with had morphed into
a young woman.

He batted away a persistent gnat and inserted the
key into the lock, wincing when he picked up the duffel. The cottage smelled like lemon oil and pine-scented
cleaner. Despite the short notice, the rental agent had
come through on her promise of getting the place
cleaned, but hints of past summers wafted around him.
He tossed his bag onto the brown leather sofa, removed
his desert camo cover and dropped the cap onto the tan
canvas duffel.

In the kitchen he checked to see if the cleaning lady
had stocked the few staples he'd requested. Sure enough,
the refrigerator had milk, eggs and cold cuts, and the
cupboards held canned goods and bread. He'd be set for
a few days. One of the reasons he'd chosen Loon Lake
was its remoteness. He'd be alone here, just him and a
couple of bottles of Jack Daniel's if his mind insisted on
tracking back to Meggie.

*I never thought you'd take advantage of my sister's
crush on you.*

Liam McBride's incensed accusations echoed in his
head like explosive antitank shells. He'd been six months
into his first deployment when Liam had left those angry
voice mails. But then five years had passed without another word.

Meggie represented his biggest regret. He could've—
no, make that should've—ended things more gently,
tried harder to make her understand. And frankly, he
should regret spending that one glorious night with her.
But he didn't.

He cursed once more under his breath. This R&R was
mandatory if he wanted to get back to the real world,

but the next thirty days stretched before him, dark and dense, like the forest blocking his view of the lake. Maybe he should've done Vegas.

A strong musty odor drew him across the kitchen to the open basement door. Before shutting it, he glanced down the stairs— What the...?

A woman sat on the bottom step, her back to him and a laundry basket on her lap, her back moving as she struggled to breathe.

"Hello? Ma'am?" Something was familiar in her movement. He took a couple steps down. "Ma'am?"

The slight figure stiffened but didn't turn around or respond. Riley clattered down the stairs, squeezing past and squatting in front of her. "Ma'am, are you—Meggie?"

His gaze froze on her green eyes, and adrenaline surged through him. What was Meg doing in his rental cabin? In his mind she'd gone on to teach elementary school in Boston. His gut clenched.

"Riley? What are you—" She began coughing and gasping, holding her chest, her wheezing more than audible.

She was sick and needed help. He commanded his emotions to stand down. "Is it your asthma?"

He'd known Meg suffered from the condition, even witnessed an attack or two in the past, but that didn't stop his stupid heart from racing.

"Just...catching...my breath." She coughed a few more times, her breathing labored. "What...are you... doing here?"

He pulled the laundry basket away and, ignoring her gasped cries of protest, tossed it aside.

"Hey, those towels were...clean." She managed to get on her feet.

He grabbed her arm to steady her. "Forget the laundry. Where's your medicine?"

God, she was prettier than he'd remembered—fantasized about—with curly red hair, green eyes with stunning flecks of hazel and gold, and thin, elegant hands, but her body now had the well-rounded curves of a woman. She dug into the pocket of her Red Sox hoodie, produced an inhaler and held it up.

As he'd done in Afghanistan, he tried to bury everything to focus on the mission. But this was more than a mission. This was Meggie. He gentled his grip on her arm. "Why aren't you using it?"

She shook the L-shaped canister and winced. "Empty."

The musty air was thin and even he had the urge to cough. "Let's get you upstairs and into some fresh air."

"Thanks." Shoving the inhaler back into her pocket, she swayed. Her wheezing had increased and she grew paler by the minute, but she eyed the basket of laundry as if she meant to bring it upstairs, too.

"I'll get that later." He studied her pale face, searching for a glimpse of the young woman he'd left behind, but this Meggie was all grown up, and her green eyes sparked with emotions he couldn't decipher.

She slapped her foot on the step just as another cough rattled through her and tipped backward, her arms flailing for the handrail.

Riley braced her against his chest, and her head hit him square in the injured shoulder, but he smothered the groan before it escaped. She steadied herself and pulled away, shaking off his hold on her arms. Grabbing the handrail, she marched up the stairs, coughing with each step. He followed close enough to catch her if she faltered again.

Upstairs he placed his hands on her shoulders and led her to the kitchen table, pulling out a chair with his foot. "Sit."

"I'm…" But she began coughing again and sank into the chair, one hand pressed flat against her chest, concern etched onto her face.

He pointed a finger. "Sit. Stay."

Her head jerked back. "Roll…over? Play d-dead?"

He grinned and she started to smile, but lost it to another cough. He threw open cupboards, impatient to find a glass. Finally locating one, he filled it with water and brought it to her, cupping her hands around it. "Drink this."

She made a noise that might have been a laugh or a cough. "What for?"

Yeah, what was it for? He ran his hand through his hair and tugged on the short strands. "I had to do something. You're…you're—"

"Trying…to breathe?" She raised her eyebrows, crinkling her forehead.

His hands fisted with the need to shake some sense into her or cradle her close and never let her go, no matter what Liam McBride or anyone said. "Do you have another inhaler at your place?"

When she shook her head, his chest squeezed in sympathy. From the moment he'd recognized Meg, he may as well have been in the blast zone from an improvised explosive device. His ears rang, his breath caught in his throat, his heart raced. Where was his battle calm? In an attempt to keep his hands to himself, he paced the small kitchen.

"I…" She set the untouched water on the table, her gaze shifting to a small purse on the counter.

How had he missed that? He grabbed the purse. "Do you have another inhaler in here?"

She shook her head. "Phone."

"Phone?" he echoed.

"To call the pharmacy…" She stood but swayed and grabbed the back of the chair before reaching for the purse he had in his hand. "For a refill."

"Meg, please. Sit down." He stepped toward her, but she waved him off. "That could take too long."

"I'll be okay in a minute." She pressed a hand to her chest.

"We shouldn't take that chance." He pulled his keys out of his pocket. "I'm taking you to the ER."

"No, really… I…" Her voice trailed off as she began gasping for air, struggling to keep upright.

"I'm done asking. Now I'm ordering." Riley put his hand under her elbow and gave her no choice. "My truck. Now."

She pulled out of his grasp. "I can…walk."

Whoa. Obviously while gaining those womanly curves, she'd lost that youthful attraction for him, but that was okay. For once something other than combat was getting his blood pumping.

Reality, meet Meg. Meg, meet reality.

This was not how her first meeting in over five years with Riley Cooper was supposed to happen. In her imagination, she was all sexy in a little black dress and killer heels after a relaxing spa day. Yeah, right; she'd spent the day cleaning and probably looked like Nick Nolte's mug shot. So not fair! Riley was supposed to be breathless and falling at her feet, not vice versa. *Stupid, stupid asthma.* Another twenty minutes and she would've been home, not making embarrassing wheezing and whistling noises in front of him.

In the cellar, Meg had thought Riley was a hallucination brought on by her oxygen-starved brain, but it hadn't taken long for her to see he was swoon-worthy flesh and blood. Riley had this whole bad-boy persona going on, with close-cropped military hair, Hollywood stubble and chiseled cheeks. What was he doing in Loon Lake? Last she knew, he was in Afghanistan. Her stomach clenched. Why had he returned?

Meg plodded toward the front door. Was it lack of oxygen or his presence making her dizzy? A million questions flitted around in her head like horseflies in spring. Forget curiosity. Giving him the third degree was out of the question until she could speak in full sentences. Another round of coughing left her light-headed. Damn, fresh air wasn't helping. She rubbed her chest, hoping to ease the new tightness settling there and chase away the black spots dancing around the edges of her vision. Every time she tried to draw in a deeper breath, the cough started again and the cycle repeated. She'd wanted to argue some more, but she could expend effort on one thing and she chose breathing.

Riley brushed past her and opened the front door.

"Wait and I'll help you into the truck." He turned back to lock the door.

A shiny black Ford F-150 hulked in the driveway. *Great, how am I supposed to climb into that beast?* "I'll manage."

He grunted and swept past, getting to the truck ahead of her. He opened the passenger door, swearing under his breath as he lifted a brown paper grocery bag off the seat. Glass bottles clinked as he turned, and she glanced into the bag. Bottles of Jack Daniel's stared back. She choked on the bitter bile rising in her throat. *Oh, God, Riley, no. Please. I don't want Fiona to come home to...this.*

Meg met his gaze. Riley's eyes resembled the lake during a summer storm. Those gray eyes—Fiona's gray eyes—dared her to say something. "Are you okay to drive?"

He lifted the bag higher, the bottles clinking and the paper bag crackling. "I haven't touched a drop. Check the bottles if you don't believe me."

"I believe you." She stepped out of his way. "Expecting company?"

"Something like that."

He set the bag on the porch steps and hustled back to the truck.

The dots dancing around the edges of her vision had increased in both size and speed, but she tried to pull herself into the pickup. Riley seized her around the waist and easily lifted her into the seat. "Thanks."

After securing her seat belt, she sat hunched forward and closed her eyes.

When he climbed behind the wheel, she pried her eyes open and eased back against the seat. "You remember... hospital?"

"Of course."

Meg tried to ignore his hand draped over the steering wheel. Not a good time for taking trips down memory lane...but those hands...

She made a strangled choking sound and turned away.

He slammed the brakes on. "Should I call an ambulance?"

"No." She motioned with her hand. "Go."

He peered at her for a moment longer before easing his foot off the brake. "Quit scaring me like that."

"Sorry." But it was his fault for looking so damn sexy. So not fair that his worn camo pants looked hot and her worn jeans looked…well, old and tattered. She wasn't wearing any makeup and Liam's old sweatshirt swallowed her whole. Yep, Meg McBride was a real sexpot. What was she doing? She needed to remember her first priority was Fiona. Riley's parting words rang in her ears. *I'm not coming back again, Meggie. The marines are my life now.* But she'd been naive enough to think she could change his mind with sex. Yeah, that worked out well. But she was in a good place in her life now and wouldn't confuse lust with love. Not that there was anything wrong with no-strings-attached sex. She might even try it…someday.

"…and I was surprised."

Oh, God. He'd been talking and she hadn't heard a word. "Sorry?"

He passed a slow-moving car. "I didn't think your family used the cottage anymore."

Was he here because he thought she wouldn't be?

"I—"

"Sorry." He glanced at her. "I didn't mean to make you keep talking. Save your breath. We can catch up later."

Fiona had two more weeks of vacation with Grampa Mac and Doris. Most lake rentals lasted a week. Riley would be gone before Fiona came home. Meg curled her fingers into her palms. She should be thinking of ways to tell Riley the truth, not celebrating the timing of his visit. If he'd come three weeks ago or two weeks from now, there would be no escaping the truth; it would be literally staring him in the face. But now? With a bag of whiskey bottles waiting on his porch? She could last a couple of weeks. Riley had shattered her heart… What would he do to Fiona's tender one?

"Meg? You still with me?"

She opened her mouth but began coughing.

"I noticed the musty smell. Did mold bring on your attack?" He turned onto the road leading to the hospital.

She reached out to rest her hand on the dashboard. "Yeah…spring rain and snowmelt caused some spring flooding."

"What about your place?" He gave her a quick glance. "Do you have mold, too?"

She nodded and he continued, "I'll take a look later and see if I can't get it cleaned up."

"No!" He gave her a wounded look and she softened her tone. "Don't waste…your week."

He slowed the truck as they approached the hospital. "No problem. I'll be here for the next thirty days."

What? Thirty days? Meg shook her head. Riley might not know—yet—what she'd done, but karma had obviously memorized it line, verse and chapter and was gleefully punishing her. First, Riley showed up looking like sex on a stick while she looked like something he'd step in with his size thirteen boots. And he was staying an entire month. Last night, after she'd talked to Fiona on the phone, Meg had cried because another fourteen days without her baby seemed like an eternity. Now, a week wasn't enough time to get ready for the impending storm.

Riley took the first empty parking spot. Her color had been pale before but it had suddenly gotten much worse.

He threw the truck into Park while the wheels were still rolling and winced when the transmission groaned.

Leaping down, he sprinted to the passenger door and pulled Meg to his side. Keeping one hand under her elbow, he hustled her through a pair of glass doors that whooshed open to a small waiting area with a nurse seated at a desk.

She greeted them with a smile, but her sharp, assessing gaze stayed on Meg. "What brings you here today?"

"Asthma. I—" A fit of coughing cut Meg off.

Riley slipped an arm across Meg's hunched shoulders, easing her closer. "She's having an asthma attack and her inhaler was empty. Ma'am, she needs to see someone. Right away."

After they'd taken seats in front of her desk, the woman tapped her finger on a small black pad that looked like a calculator. "Can you type your Social Security number into this for me?"

After Meg typed in her number, the nurse slipped a blood pulse oximeter on her finger.

"When did the wheezing start?" the nurse asked and verified Meg's date of birth and social.

"About…thirty minutes ago." Meg leaned forward in the seat.

"And what were you doing?"

"Laundry."

Riley drew his chair closer and secured an arm around Meg as if she'd slip away from him if he let go. He listened impatiently to every inane question and Meg's breathless replies, the incessant tapping on the keypad. Geez, couldn't they just give her an inhaler or something? What was taking so long?

The nurse checked the oximeter and clucked her

tongue. "Ninety-one. We'll get you back there right away."

While the nurse put a hospital bracelet around Meg's wrist, Riley glanced over at the crowded waiting room. Texting and watching TV, none of them looked as though they wanted to shout and tear the place apart until their loved one was treated. Not that Meg was…

He closed his eyes and rubbed his forefinger across the bridge of his nose, searching for calm. He'd been fighting nausea since finding her at the bottom of those stairs. Sheer force of will had kept him moving up to this moment. Sweat trickled down his sides. Meg had asked him if he'd been expecting company when he'd picked up his bag of Jack Daniel's bottles. What he hadn't told her was that most nights the image of Private Trejo lying in a pool of blood and spilled guts at the bottom of those dusty steps in Kandahar kept him company.

A hand touched his arm, and his eyes flew open.

"She's going to be fine." The nurse flashed a reassuring smile. "Someone is coming right out to get her."

The door to the ER buzzed open and another nurse in dark blue scrubs stepped through, pushing a wheelchair in front of her. She called for Meg. Riley swallowed and helped Meg stand.

"Meg, I figured that must be you when I saw the name on the face sheet from triage." The trim, fortysomething nurse glanced at him, did a double take and smiled. "I would say it's good to see you, but considering we're in the ER, I won't."

"Hi, Jan. I'd…" Meg coughed and settled in the chair, and Riley started to follow them into a small treatment area. "I'd say the same, but yeah, ER and all."

Jan stopped and gave him a sharp look. "Are you a relative?"

"No." *But if you think you're keeping me out here and away from Meggie, think again, lady.*

"He's…" Meg's gaze bounced between him and Jan. "I'd like him with me."

The nurse nodded and started forward again. He sighed, glad he didn't have to fight and claw his way back there to be sure they did their best for Meg.

"We'll get you fixed up right quick," Jan said cheerfully as she wheeled Meg down a short hall with curtained treatment areas. "I ran into Brody the other day at the Pic-N-Save. He said Fiona is enjoying her trip. Bet you miss her like crazy. It was the Grand Canyon, wasn't it?"

Meg bit her lower lip. "Yes. Grand Canyon."

"They went by motor home, didn't they?"

"Yes." Meg's fingers gripped the sides of the chair, her knuckles white.

Riley looked to Meg, but she ignored him. Who was Fiona and why would Meg be missing her *like crazy*? And who was Brody?

She's made a life for herself complete with new friends in the past five years, dumbass.

The nurse stopped in front of a curtained treatment area, engaged the brake on the wheelchair and helped Meg transfer to a narrow stretcher. She closed the curtain and pulled a hospital gown from an overhead cabinet. "Sir, if you'll wait on the other side of the curtain for a moment."

"Yes, ma'am." He was loath to leave Meg, but took a step back. Getting escorted out by security wouldn't be a good idea.

"Thanks." The nurse smiled at him as she yanked the curtain closed in his face. "Now, Meg, take off your shirt and unhook your bra."

The curtain hadn't closed all the way and he could still see Meg. He should be a gentleman about this. But he needed to reassure himself they were taking proper care of Meg. *Yeah, right.*

Jan, the nurse, clucked her tongue, saying, "Oh, my." Riley stiffened as she continued, "Looks like you've got some mold on the back of this sweatshirt."

"I must've brushed up against it in the basement," Meg responded.

"I'll bag the shirt up just as a precaution and look for a scrub top for you to wear home," Jan said and there was some rustling.

"There, all covered," Jan said, as if signaling the all clear, and Riley stepped back around the curtain.

A tech came in right behind him and took Meg's vital signs while the nurse did an evaluation. He clenched his jaw. How many questions did they have to ask before they treated her?

The curtain flew aside and the doctor stepped in, stethoscope looped around his neck and holding a clipboard. He introduced himself and pulled a small black stool up to the stretcher and sat down.

"So you've had an asthma attack. Was this one any worse than the others?"

"No, but I had used up my inhaler and *someone* got a little freaked out."

Riley opened his mouth but thought better of arguing and shut it again.

"I see. Let's have a listen." The doctor stuck his stethoscope under the gown and listened to Meg's chest, right upper, left upper, right lower, then left lower, then repeating the process on her back all the while explaining, "We're going to get your asthma exacerbation under control by giving you several updrafts back to back and, if necessary, an IV steroid."

When he finished, he went to the computer to document his findings and the nurse tied the gown. "It says you have inhalers. Did you say you used one today?"

Unable to keep silent any longer, Riley stepped away from the wall he'd been leaning against. "The one she had was empty. I found her at—"

"And you are?" The doctor turned and studied Riley over the top of his glasses.

Riley flexed his fingers. Good question. What was he to Meg? Blowing out the breath he'd been holding in, he said, "Riley Cooper, sir."

The doctor glanced at the chart. "Are you a relative?"

Riley stepped closer to Meg. "I'm—"

"He's just, uh…just a neighbor."

Well, that answered who and what he was. His gut burned at being relegated to such a mundane role in Meg's life.

Chapter Two

"Meg gave her permission for him to be here," Jan said into the silence.

Meg rubbed her nose and avoided eye contact with Riley, but sneaked a look at his arms folded over his well-defined chest. And yes, she knew that chest was rock-hard from when he'd caught her on the stairs.

Good grief, what was she thinking, and more to the point, why was he back here after all this time? Just her luck to have an asthma attack in the middle of cleaning up the place for—of all people—Riley. Why had she let him talk her into coming to the ER? And why had she assumed the mold in that basement had been cleaned up in the first place? If she'd known how bad it was, she would've refused the job. Or at least refilled the inhaler before going.

She needed to be paying attention to the doctor, but

Riley's looming presence dwarfed everyone and everything else. Well, he couldn't overwhelm her now. His surprise appearance at the cottage had flustered her and thrown her back into the old habit of thinking he hung the moon. That's the explanation she had for letting him bully her into coming to the hospital. But she was an adult with a good life in Loon Lake and was working hard to provide Fiona with the security every child deserved. Riley might be sexier than ever, but she couldn't let him in. Not after he'd made it plain his presence was temporary. She had to assume the marines were still his passion, his first choice. He'd shattered her heart and she wouldn't allow him to do that to Fiona. Meg's job as Fiona's mom was not only to provide but also to protect.

And yet, hadn't she hurt Fiona by keeping her existence a secret from Riley? Hiding a child wasn't pay back, no matter what Riley had done. Fiona had every right to know her father, and vice versa. He'd ignored her letters, but she'd planned on swallowing her pride and doing what was necessary to contact him…right up until the day that manila envelope had arrived. In it were her letters to him. He'd returned every damn one—unopened.

"Let's adjust this a bit," Jan muttered as she fiddled with the oxygen mask.

The movement, as much as the increased oxygen, jerked Meg back to the present.

The doctor scribbled a note and spoke to the nurse. "We need to see about getting Meghan a room for the night."

Wait, what? A room? As in hospitalized overnight? *No, no, no.* With her high deductible insurance plan, she'd be in debt until Fiona left for college—longer. Meg sat straighter and tugged the mask down. "No. I can't stay over—"

"You need this." Riley settled the mask firmly back in place.

She tried to slap his hand away, but he wouldn't budge.

The doctor cleared his throat. "It's a precaution. I don't think you should be alone tonight, Meghan."

Riley released his hold on the mask. "I'll stay with her."

Meg shook her head. Fiona's presence covered every inch of their home. She couldn't deal with this tonight. The asthma treatments would leave her jittery and grouchy. Her dream of slinky dresses and killer heels might be dead, but she still needed some type of armor when she dealt with Riley.

"According to this, you were doing laundry when the attack occurred." The doctor frowned. "I see mold is one of your triggers, so I assume there's mold at your place?"

She groaned inwardly. If she said yes, the doctor would want her to stay in the hospital. If she said no, Riley would insist on staying at her place. It was a no-win situation. Maybe being in debt for the rest of her life wouldn't be so bad. Ramen noodles weren't the worst things in the world.

"My cottage is next to hers and it's my understanding, sir, both basements flooded." Riley laid his hand on her shoulder.

Meg tried to shrug it off and failed. The warmth of his fingers was scrambling her brain because she had an urge to lean into his strength. She was doing fine on her own. With her graduation from college this semester and her successful completion of student teaching last semester, she'd sent the letter of disposition required for teacher certification. Once she received certification, she could pursue a full-time position. No more cleaning cottages to pick up extra cash between subbing jobs. Sure, she'd had some setbacks with her unreliable car and the flooded basement, but nothing she couldn't handle, and she'd already applied for a fall teaching job. Speed bumps were a part of life, but the bag with bottles of whiskey on Riley's porch could signal more than a bump in the road for Fiona. He hadn't been a drinker before he left so Meg had been surprised by the alcohol, but that proved she didn't know Riley anymore and her job was to protect her daughter.

The doctor removed his glasses and slipped them in his shirt pocket. "Under normal circumstances, having some mold in the cellar wouldn't put you in undue stress, but a second response to the same trigger would be twice as bad."

"I'm taking her to a motel for tonight." Riley squeezed her shoulder. "And I'll be sure her basement gets cleaned up."

"Sounds good." The doctor stood and pushed the stool back. He shook Riley's hand and patted Meg's leg. "I'll discharge you if you stay away from any triggers at least for tonight and use your nebulizer every four hours. Don't hesitate to return if your condition worsens during the night. And be sure to fill your inhaler prescription."

Meg sputtered. What made Riley think he could show up and take over? She was capable of taking care of her daughter, herself and her home, thank you very much. After her ma had died, she'd discovered a strength she hadn't known she possessed. She'd taken care of everything after her father and brother fell apart, and she'd been barely out of her teens, all the while caring for an infant and working to finish college. She'd been handling things for a long time now and she'd—

"Keep that oxygen on while I go to see about your paperwork," Jan said and sneaked a glance at Riley before sweeping past the curtain, her sneakers squeaking on the polished floor.

Just like that it was a done deal. Meg made a grab for the mask, but Riley stopped her. "What part of *keep this on* did you not understand?"

Fine. She'd talk through the stupid mask. "You don't have to go to any trouble. I can take care of myself and see that my basement is cleaned up."

He bent over her, one hand resting next to her head, the other near her hip. "Tonight I issue orders. You follow them."

Before she could form a protest, he leaned closer. Dear Lord, was he going to kiss her? Her heart beat erratically and her eyes closed, as if she'd lost control of them. His firm lips touched her forehead. What did he think he was doing? How dare he! How…how… Her protests went unspoken as she tried to process his actions. Riley had kissed her. A peck on her forehead, but she'd liked it. Oh, God, she'd liked it. She had plans and Riley Cooper was not part of those. At one time he had been, but then she'd tried to tell him about Fiona and he hadn't bothered to open, let alone read, her letters. But what about those dreams of finding someone to share all of life's ups and downs? She shoved those thoughts aside. Why go looking for trouble or heartache?

Jan moved the curtain, jangling the rings against the metal rod. Riley straightened and stepped back. Great, now it would be all over town that Meg McBride not only sent her daughter away so she could carry on a raging affair with a hot stranger but ended up in the ER with him. A story begging for embellishment.

"Let's get you ready to go." Jan dropped a stack of papers next to Meg's feet and bustled around, unhooking the oxygen and handing Meg the bra, T-shirt and her hoodie safely sealed in a plastic bag.

Riley straightened up and stepped away from the stretcher. "Ma'am, could you direct me to the nearest head…uh, restroom?"

"The head? Are you saying I run a tight ship?" Jan laughed.

Riley grinned. "Land or sea it's the same to a grunt."

She stepped into the hall. "I prefer the tight ship theory, but here, let me get you started in the right direction."

Meg began dressing while Jan was giving Riley directions. Her fingers shook as she tried to get the bra on and she knew the shakes weren't entirely due to the asthma meds. Try as she might, she couldn't block out the fact that Riley had kissed her. She should be furious with him. So why wasn't she?

"Here, let me help." Jan helped her get the hooks threaded into the loops. "I must say, everyone is admiring your…uh…um…"

"He's a friend of Liam's and just happens to be renting the cottage next to mine." Meg left out the part how Riley had sometimes spent summers as a child at the lake with his parents and then later as a guest of her family. That was close to ten years ago; no need to remind everyone of a silly childhood crush she'd gotten over a long time ago.

"Yeah, Lorena down at the Pic-N-Save said a hottie in a big black pickup had stopped for gas at that shiny new station off the interstate at the same time she was fueling up." Jan straightened the papers she'd left on the bed. "Lorena was asking everyone who came in if they knew anything about him. Won't those girls be jealous when they find out I know something they don't."

"Mmm." Meg pulled the cotton scrub top over her head.

"Oh, but look at me. Goodness, I shouldn't be talking about your…uh, friend like that." Jan helped Meg pull her hair from beneath the shirt.

"He's my brother's friend," Meg said through gritted teeth. Who was she trying to convince…them or herself?

Jan picked up the papers. "Yes. Yes. Of course. Your…um, Riley said he'd meet you at the nurses' station."

Meg sighed. Her life would be a lot simpler if everyone would just stay out of her business.

Riley thanked the young, dark-haired nurse at the desk. While the one motel in Loon Lake was closed for renovations, she'd suggested one not too far away and had even called to check availability.

With the room booked, now all Riley had to do was get Meg there. He knew she'd fight him on it, but he wasn't letting her go back to either cottage tonight, nor was he leaving her alone. As far as he knew, her dad and brother were living three hours away in Boston. He might not want to admit it, but she'd scared him. And he'd been in some terrifying situations during his time in the sandbox. When he returned to his men, he wanted to do it knowing Meg was here in Loon Lake, safe and happy.

And is that your explanation for your boneheaded behavior back there, Marine?

The kiss had been spontaneous and it was a toss-up who'd been more surprised by the gesture. For a split second, the emotions he'd bottled up had threatened to consume him. He'd been afraid she'd pass out or worse before he could get her help. But he was glad he'd been there, able to help her, and that he'd finally helped someone rather than watching them die.

Look on the bright side, Marine—giving her a quick peck was preferable to clinging to her in relief.

"Here's your confirmation number." The nurse handed him a yellow sticky note.

He shifted the bag in his hand and took the paper. "Thanks...uh..."

She blushed. "Ellie."

"Appreciate it, Ellie." He turned toward the footsteps coming down the hall and went to meet Meg.

He thanked God Meg's color had returned, but those bruising circles under her eyes and the oversize scrub top gave her a fragile appearance. His gut clenched as he fought the urge to scoop her up and carry her off. *To where? The nearest cave?* Had he lost his mind? He had obligations that didn't include Meg and he needed to remember that.

Meg pointed to the white plastic bag in his hand. "Been shopping?"

"I heard the nurse say there was mold on your hoodie and it's getting chillier out there." He pulled a pink hooded sweatshirt from the bag and a teddy bear fell out, but he caught the stuffed animal before it landed on the floor.

She raised her eyebrows at the bear but didn't say

anything, and he regretted his impulse buy. *And you thought this was a good idea why, Marine?*

"Here," he muttered and handed her the bear.

"What's this for?" Her glance bounced between him and the toy.

"It's to replace the one Liam and I used for archery practice." He cleared his throat. "I've…uh, been meaning to replace it for a long time now."

Her eyes narrowed. "I knew you two had something to do with it."

"I wanted to tell you but Liam threatened me." He shoved his hands in the pockets of his cammies.

The corners of her mouth twitched up. "Threatened you? With what? You were always bigger than him."

"He said he'd end our friendship."

"Liam's friendship meant that much to you?"

"Being with your family meant that much to me." His time with the McBrides had been his escape when things got ugly between his parents. Meg's family talked to him without giving him the third degree, expecting him to rat out the other parent, depending on which one was asking. At Christmas, while the McBrides gathered around their tree, he'd been dragged to destinations one parent had picked to make it difficult for the other to visit. Now his relationship with them had devolved into awkwardly polite phone calls on birthdays and holidays.

She lifted a tag attached to the bear's ear. "I don't believe it."

"What?" Did he leave the price tag on?

"It says his name is Jasper." She sounded incredulous.

"That's what made me think of it."

"You remembered my bear's name was Jasper?" she whispered and her eyes lit up.

"I wanted to fix it and give it back to you, but I had no clue how, and anyway Liam would've known it was me…" He shrugged.

She gave him a smile that made the embarrassment worth it.

They'd reached the nurses' station and Meg signed the paperwork, took the small bag of meds Jan handed her and began marching toward the exit before his brain kicked back into gear. With a nod to the nurses gawking at him from behind the counter, he caught up to Meg and placed his hand against the small of her back.

"Why was she giving you her phone number?" Meg increased her pace, but his stride was longer and he easily kept up and maintained contact as they exited the building.

"Who?" He pulled his keys out of his pocket with his free hand, the other still planted against her back.

"Ellie Harding. I saw her giving you that slip of paper." She tossed her hair over her shoulder and settled the teddy bear in the crook of her arm.

She must mean the confirmation number. Where was she going with this? "What paper?"

"The one you put in your pocket." She stopped short, but he managed not to mow her down. "Don't try to deny it. I saw it."

"According to you, all I am is a neighbor." He kept his tone casual, not wanting her to know how she'd hurt him by denying their connection. "So why would you even care?"

"Pfft." She restarted her brisk pace through the parking lot. "I don't."

"And yet you mentioned it."

She shook her head. "Forget I said anything."

He opened the passenger door. "That's hard to do since you insist on talking about it."

"I'm not talking."

"Then what is that thing you're doing with your mouth?" He cocked an eyebrow, knowing his ability to lift one would bug her. She'd been around twelve when he'd caught her practicing in front of a mirror, trying and failing to imitate him by raising just one eyebrow. He shouldn't be goading her, but falling back into their good-natured teasing felt good and helped melt away some of the distance the years had wedged between them.

She rolled her eyes at him, and the rays from the sun sitting low on the horizon fell on her face, causing the amber ring circling her pupils to glow. He'd never met another woman with eyes as beautifully sexy as hers.

"I love your eyes." He hadn't meant to say that, but the words had catapulted from his mouth like a fighter jet off the deck of a carrier. He might not have set out to say anything like that, but he wasn't sorry.

"Wha-what?"

Placing his thumb under her jaw, he closed her mouth. "I was remarking on your eyes."

She stuck her chin out. "The medical term is sectoral heterochromia."

He understood what she was saying, or rather, what she wasn't saying. Her reaction reminded him of his when the doctors talked about his survivor's guilt. "People like to label things."

"Kids made fun. Said I had freckles in my eyes. Except—" she clutched the bear tighter, but didn't look away "—you. You never did."

"I was too busy teasing you about this red hair." He ran his fingers through the soft, springy curls.

"It's not red." She glared at him, but her lips twitched, telling him she wasn't angry. "It's golden copper. How many times do I have to tell you that?"

"Golden copper, huh?" He wrapped a curl around his index finger, gave a gentle tug and let go, grinning when the corkscrew sprang back. "Sure looks red to me."

"Well, there's a difference." She brushed the hair off her face. "And you'd know that if you'd been paying attention."

"Oh, I paid attention, Meggie. As a matter of fact, I—"

An ambulance, its sirens blaring and lights flashing, passed and he followed its progress as it pulled under the portico of the emergency entrance. When he turned back, she was watching the ambulance, her brows drawn together over the bridge of her nose. He smoothed his thumb over the deep grooves. "Let's go."

"Yes, please." She nodded and turned back to him. "Take me home."

He *tsked* his tongue. "No. Can. Do."

Her eyes widened. "But you just said—"

"I said we're leaving here. If *you'd* been paying attention, you'd know I didn't specify a destination." He opened the passenger door. "Remember, I'm under doctor's orders to take you to a motel tonight."

"What? Why that's…that's… No. Take me home."

He risked an elbow in his stomach but hovered as she pulled herself into the truck. Once she was seated, he grinned and said, "Can't. The doc and I shook on it and everything."

"Why… I… You…"

"Hold that thought." He slammed the door and hustled around the front of the truck. Getting under her skin felt good. Too good. His hand tightened around his key. He had men counting on him to return at 100 percent. If he wasn't careful, the one woman he couldn't get out of his system might distract him from that goal.

When was the last time someone had left her speechless? Meg buckled her seat belt with a loud click. She brushed her hand over the bear's plush fur. If she wasn't careful, Riley would crawl right back into her heart. She needed to remember he was here for thirty days, and as a single mother to an impressionable little girl, she couldn't do temporary.

And she wasn't going to look at his hands on the steering wheel...she wasn't. She— *Damn*. Her short nails dug into the palms of her hands and her mother's words echoed in her head. *You need to be careful how much attention you pay to that boy. He'll get the wrong idea about what kind of girl you are.*

Sorry, Ma, but he got the wrong idea. But now she was on a good path, a smart path and—

"I can hear you all the way over here."

"What?" She jerked her head back, warmth spreading across her cheeks. "I didn't say anything."

"No, but you're busy thinking it." He draped his hand over the wheel, giving her a sidelong glance and a devilish grin.

If he wasn't the most annoying... She sighed. No other man in her acquaintance sparked her nerve endings the way Riley did. Not that Loon Lake was crawling with eligible men, but enough to convince her that what she felt for Riley didn't come along every day. "I wasn't thinking anything."

"Just like you weren't talking?" He glanced over and quirked his eyebrow.

Meg sighed and shifted in the seat. Ugh. He used that one eyebrow like a sexy weapon, as if he knew that simple action tied her in knots.

"I was— Hey, you missed the turn." She dragged in a tight breath. Good heavens, was he serious about a motel?

He gave her a dimpled grin. "I told you. We're going to a motel."

Those dang dimples—yeah, more ammo in his sex-on-a-stick arsenal. She shook her head. "I'm not going anywhere dressed like this."

"Sorry, but you've already been somewhere dressed like that."

"Well, thank you, Captain Obvious." She turned her head toward the passenger-side window. As if the asthma meds hadn't made her squirrely enough, the sight of his hands had her squirming. "But that was an emergency."

"Ah, but the motel is an extension of the original mission." Slowing for a red light, he turned his head to study her. "Marines don't stop until the job is finished."

"You got the job done. I can breathe and—" she rattled her bag "—I have more meds if anything happens."

"You heard the doctor. No exposure to mold tonight." The light changed and he drove through the intersection. "Afraid you won't be able to resist me?"

She snorted. "Oh, please. If anything, I'm more likely to strangle you in your sleep."

"Hmm…" He wiggled both eyebrows at her. "Considering you'd have to climb on top of me to have that sort of access."

As if she needed *that* picture in her head. "I'm serious, Riley."

He leaned sideways toward her. "So am I. I plan to stick to you like a foul odor."

She rolled her eyes. "Which reminds me. I need a shower. I spent the whole day cleaning that cottage."

He grinned, all white teeth and dimples peeking out from the stubble. "You can shower at the motel."

She still had an ace up her sleeve and brought out her sweetest, fakest smile. "But these clothes have mold and dust and who knows what clinging to them. You heard the doctor. No more exposure means I need clean clothes."

"That nurse gave you a top to wear."

"Yeah, but what about the rest of my clothes? My sneakers and—"

"You've made your point. I should've remembered you don't play fair." He barked out a laugh, but pulled onto the shoulder of the road. "We'll get whatever you need and you can argue with me all you want, but we're still going to a motel."

She swallowed hard, remembering the last time they'd ended up in a motel room together.

"Why were you cleaning the cottage?" He checked for traffic before easing back onto the road.

"I was repaying a favor." She shrugged. "I guess karma didn't get that part of the message."

"Yeah, good deeds and all that." He completed the U-turn and sped up. "So you're living in Loon Lake full-time?"

"Yup, I'm a permanent resident." Tomorrow, when

the worst of the asthma meds were out of her system, would be time enough for the rest of the story. She had her application in with the school system, where she'd done her student teaching. She wouldn't let Riley's sexy dimples blind her to her priorities. She had a daughter to raise, a career to start and a life to live.

"Living at your dad's place makes it convenient."

"Except it's not my dad's place." She was proud of owning a home and wanted to make sure he knew about it. "It's mine. I own it."

"Really?" His eyes widened. "You took the place on by yourself?"

That's nothing. I lost my mother, nursed my broken heart and had your baby all by myself. "Don't sound so surprised. In case you hadn't noticed, I grew up while you were gone."

He turned toward her, his gaze sweeping over her. "Oh, I noticed. All I'm saying is the winters can be harsh. That alone would create a lot of upkeep."

"I can handle it… I *am* handling it." Okay, so she was going to have to prioritize her projects due to her car dying and the flooding. Homes on the other end of the lake and ones right on the water had it worse, so she considered herself lucky.

"Your dad wasn't interested in keeping the place for retirement?"

"No, he signed the deed over to Liam and me. I bought my brother out." She had grabbed the chance to own a home and raise Fiona in a small town noted for its excellent school system. Here, they had a yard where Meg planned to put up a swing set and, as soon as she found an affordable one that didn't set off her asthma, she'd get Fiona a puppy. "Neither one of them had much interest in the place after Mom died."

Riley cleared his throat. "I was sorry to hear about your mother's death. By the time word got to me in the sandbox, it was too late. I wish I could've been there for you, Meg."

"Thanks, but I didn't expect you." But that hadn't prevented her from searching each new face that came through the door.

"How has Mac been doing?"

"He's doing great. He's remarried and—"

"Wait. Mac remarried? Wow, I…" He shook his head. "I guess that shows how long I've been gone."

She clenched her jaw. *And totally cut us out of your life while you were at it.* "You've been gone for nearly six years."

"Sorry, didn't mean to interrupt." He reached over and squeezed her hand. "Tell me about Mac."

The calluses were new…and sexy. Oh, God, she needed to stop this. Riley might press all her buttons, but she needed to remember that whiskey on his porch. Needed to remember their chemistry wasn't enough to bind him to her. She'd tried that and failed. Their one night together bound her to him in the form of their daughter, but he didn't know that…yet. "As I was saying, a widow moved in next door about two years ago and they hit it off right away. They got married at the end of last year when Dad retired."

"Mac retired? I thought they'd have to wheel him out of the fire station." He rubbed his thumb over her knuckles. "Do you like his new wife?"

"I like her very much. Doris is sweet and she's been a great…" She hesitated.

"Great what?"

"Influence on my dad." She'd been going to say "grand-mother," but this wasn't the time or place for *that* explanation. "Getting him to retire and all."

Riley squeezed her hand. "Is it hard watching him with someone else?"

"A little at first, but I'm glad he's happy."

"What about you, Meggie? Are *you* happy living here?"

"Yes, I am," she said and meant it. She'd taken a chance thirteen months ago, uprooting Fiona from Boston to settle in Loon Lake, but they'd made a life for themselves in the quintessential New England town. The wood-covered bridge, pre-Revolutionary War architecture and town green with summer band concerts in the gazebo were the things the tourists saw, but Meg knew firsthand about the caring and kind people who inhabited Loon Lake. Fiercely independent, they never asked for help and yet assisted anyone one who might need it. She still wasn't sure who to thank for making sure her driveway was plowed after each snowstorm last winter.

Here she could give Fiona community and recreational opportunities that might have been out of reach in Boston. She glanced at Riley, wondering what it would be like to share this life she'd made with him.

She pushed that thought aside, too tired to deal with the enormity of it tonight and the role she and her wounded pride had played in keeping father and daughter apart. She regretted that decision, but it was too late to take it back. All she could do now was hope Fiona didn't pay the price for her selfishness.

Call me Scarlett, but I'll worry about that tomorrow.

* * *

Riley stopped his truck in front of Meg's place, glad she had no idea what he was thinking. Of course, she couldn't call him any names worse than those he'd called himself during the drive from the hospital. Every time she'd shifted in her seat, he responded, thinking how she'd felt underneath him that night, how no other woman since had made him feel so special.

Nice going, Marine. The woman has a life-threatening asthma attack and all you can think about is jumping her bones.

But then he laughed to himself because that was pretty much the number one objective for a marine on leave.

Meg was white picket fences and family dinners on Sunday, and he was forward operating bases and MREs. She needed someone who was emotionally stable and re-liable, not someone chasing an adrenaline rush in the lat-est battle zone. Putting the truck in Park and killing the engine, he said, "Tell me what you want and I'll get it."

"What I want is to stay home. I've lived with asthma all my life. I can take care of myself."

She could fight him all she wanted, but she was stay-ing in the motel tonight if he had to put her over his shoulder. He was keeping her safe at all costs. No more deaths on his watch. Or his conscience. "So why did I find you at the bottom of the stairs, gasping for air?"

"It wasn't that bad. I was catching my breath before climbing back upstairs."

"Yeah, well, life sucks. You're coming with me to the motel. I came here because you said you wanted to get a change of clothes. You can do that or we'll leave right now." He hated sounding like such a hard-ass, but he wasn't taking any chances with Meg's safety, so he restarted the truck's engine as a demonstration.

"All right. All right." She unbuckled her seat belt, filling the cab with that insistent pinging noise. "But I go in and get my own stuff. I don't want you pawing through my things."

"Afraid of what I might find hidden in your underwear drawer?" He raised his eyebrows.

"Don't you have something on your front porch that *you* need to bring inside?"

"Touché." Earlier, he'd toyed with the idea of getting acquainted with one of those bottles tonight, but now he wasn't taking any chances. He needed to be alert in case she had a relapse. "I'll go take care of my *stuff* while you get what you need."

He cut the engine again and she scrambled out of the truck. Her swaying hips and cute butt presented a nice view, lightening his mood without the threat of a hangover.

Remember, returning to your squad was the original mission, Marine.

"And don't forget to come back out. Locking your door won't stop me, Meggie. I'm very good at gaining access to barricaded buildings," he called after her.

She paused on her way up the porch steps to look over her shoulder. "You would come in, knowing you weren't welcome?"

He barked out a laugh. "I've spent much of the past six years in Afghanistan. I'm used to being where I'm not welcome."

He loped across the distance separating their houses. Putting his bag of clanking bottles on the floor inside the door, he opened his gear bag and pulled out a bottle of ibuprofen. This was the only painkiller he was allowing himself tonight. He grabbed the duffel off the couch and grunted at the twinge in his shoulder. If lucky, Meg wouldn't force him to take extreme measures to get her to the motel.

To his surprise, and his shoulder's relief, she was waiting next to his truck with an overnight case. He lifted his chin toward her bag. "Your nebulizer better be in there."

She rolled those beautiful eyes at him, but nodded. *Oorah*. He might be calculating Red Sox batting averages in his head before this night was over, but for now he'd savor his victory.

Checking into their room at the motel ran so smoothly, he suspected Meg had run out of steam. She hadn't even given him more than token grief over sharing a room. Once inside, she threw her overnight case on one of the double beds, pulled out some items and headed for the bathroom.

"Calling dibs," was all she said before shutting the door. The lock engaged with a click that echoed.

Despite the utilitarian pressboard furniture, brown tweed carpet, ugly orange drapes and matching bed covers, the room was spotless.

The shower came on and images of a naked Meg filled his head. He fisted his hands at the thought of exploring those new curves. Barely out of her teens when he'd last seen her, she'd been coltish, all legs and arms. But now...

With a muttered curse at the direction of his thoughts, he grabbed the television remote, flipping through channels until he found a baseball game. Not that he'd be able to concentrate, but at least he'd try. Lying on one of the beds, he pretended the game interested him.

The water switched off and he swung his legs off the bed and stood. Clearing his throat, he went closer to the door. "I was thinking of ordering a pizza. You interested?"

"Yeah…o-okay sure."

She didn't sound sure and—

Damn. How could he have forgotten they'd fed one another pizza that night? He rubbed his palms on his pants. "Look, there's a burger joint down the road. I can—"

"Pizza is fine."

Riley ordered and waited for her to finish with the blow-dryer before approaching the bathroom door again. "I'm going to get us some drinks from the vending machine."

"Okay. Thanks."

Riley took his time, hoping the fresh air would clear his head a bit. His imagination kept conjuring up images of Meg naked on the other side of that bathroom door.

He heard her talking to someone when he got back to the room and quietly pushed the door open.

Dressed in a blue fuzzy robe, she had her back to him, holding her cell phone to her ear. "I told you I'm fine. I called because I knew you'd eventually hear about it anyway. No, Liam, you do *not* need to talk to him. I'm a big girl. I can handle this."

Riley set the cans on the small table, but she didn't turn around.

"Oh, for heaven's sake, you do *not* need to come up here. And no, don't call Dad. He'll just worry and that will worry Fiona. You know what kind of radar she has."

Meg shifted from one foot to the other. "No, I don't want them to cut their trip short. Stay out of this."

She turned around as if realizing he was back in the room. Shaking her head and rolling her eyes, she said, "Don't make me regret calling you. I'm fine and if you tell, I'll hunt you down. You know I will…Yeah, love you, too."

Slipping the phone into the front pocket on her robe, she tightened the belt. "I figured I'd better call Liam before he heard about my ER visit from someone else."

"Would word reach him one hundred and sixty miles away in Boston?"

She shook her head. "You'd be surprised."

A knock at the door signaled their pizza delivery before Riley could say anything more. He opened the door and huffed out a laugh. Was this kid even old enough to drive? "Hey. How much?"

"It's…" The boy paused as he glanced over Riley's shoulder. Then his eyes widened and his jaw dropped. "Ms. McBride? Is that you? Really you?"

"Kevin?" Meg's voice rose, along with the color in her cheeks.

Riley glanced over his shoulder at Meggie. *Ms. Mc-Bride?* Dear Lord, he had been gone a long time.

Riley tried to take the pizza box, but the kid had it in a tight grip. What the…? The teen, his expression a mixture of shock and disappointment, stared at Meg. Whoa, he had a crush on Meg and was reacting to finding her in a motel room with some guy. Poor kid. "Kevin, is it?"

The teen turned his attention back to Riley. "Uh, yeah, Kevin Thompson."

"Pleasure to meet you, Kevin." Riley clapped him on the shoulder since Kevin's hands were full of pizza box.

"Meg—uh, Ms. McBride had an asthma attack and we agreed with the doctor's recommendation that she not be exposed to the mold in her basement until we can get it cleaned up."

Kevin's eyes widened. "Oh, hey, I— You're okay now, though, right, Ms. McBride?"

"Yes, I'm feeling much better now, thank you." Meg stepped closer. "I'm glad to see Bert gave you the job."

"Thanks to you." The kid ducked his head. "The way you vouched for me and all…uh…thanks."

"You're welcome." Meg pointed a finger at him and spoke in a motherly tone. "Just be sure your grades don't suffer."

"Oh, no, I promise because I really… I mean…" The kid glanced down and shuffled his feet.

Riley lifted the box from Kevin's hands, set it on the table and decided to go with his gut. "Kevin, I might need some help with the cleanup in Meg's—Ms. McBride's—basement. Would you be available to help?"

"Yes, sir, I sure would." Kevin bobbled his head, his attention now on Riley. "Are you like the one that's in the marines?"

News did travel fast in Loon Lake, or maybe it was different now that Meg lived here full-time. He hadn't paid attention to gossip when he'd been here as a kid. "That's right. I'm a marine."

Meg cleared her throat. "Won't Bert be waiting on you, Kevin?"

"Oh, yeah, that's right. I should get back there. Glad you're feeling better." The teen turned to leave.

"Wait." Riley pressed some bills into Kevin's hand. "Don't want to forget to pay you for the pizza and have you be responsible."

The boy glanced at the money. "Oh, hey, but that's way too—"

"Keep it." Riley shrugged. "We kept you here talking when you could've been collecting more tips."

The kid shoved the wadded bills into his pocket. "Uh, yeah, sure. Thanks, man. And if you need help with the basement…"

"I'll be in touch after I make an initial inspection," Riley told him.

"Sure, sure." Kevin nodded. "Well, uh…have a nice night."

"Stay safe," Meg called as Riley shut the door and flipped the dead bolt.

Riley turned and stared at her. "*Ms.* McBride?"

Her mouth twitched. "I did my student teaching at the high school."

"I think you have an admirer." He playfully bumped shoulders.

"If you ask me, he had a few stars in his eyes when he looked at you." She grinned.

"Seems like a decent kid," Riley remarked as he flipped open the pizza box, filling the air with the scent of warm dough and pepperoni.

"He is. Kevin's had it rough, but I think he's on the right path."

"Bad home life?" After Riley's parents split, each had used him as a weapon against the other. He'd hated getting shuttled from one to the other, hated new people coming into his life for short periods of time, then disappearing as each parent dated and, most of all, he'd hated the emotional void he'd had to endure as they got so caught up in their own pain and they'd ignored his.

The marines had given him the structure and the sense of belonging he'd craved as a child.

"Kevin's mom left when he was young. His dad is rarely sober and often out of work." Meg rubbed a finger across one eyebrow. "Kevin was left to his own devices."

"That's gotta be rough. He's lucky he has you to look out for him." He set a pizza slice on a napkin and pushed it toward her before taking one for himself.

Imagine, his little Meggie an authority figure to teenagers. His chest tightened. What else had he missed? "Looks like you've made a place for yourself in the Loon Lake community."

"And all the stuff that goes with it." She heaved a sigh and sank into the wooden chair at the small round table, reaching for one of the sodas he'd bought.

He frowned. "Problem?"

"Between the ER and now the motel, gossip will be circling around Loon Lake like Martin Evers's homing pigeons." She pulled the soda can tab with a sharp snap and laughed. "I wish my real life was as interesting as the one everyone will be talking about."

He settled into the seat opposite her. "I don't see the harm, you're an adult. And Kevin proved it by calling you Ms. McBride."

"Yeah, still getting used to that part." She shook her head. "Still, I would prefer not to be the subject of gossip."

"It's pretty harmless." He folded his slice in half lengthwise and took a bite.

"I… I have more than myself to think of." She ran her fingertip along the ridge of the soda can.

Riley chewed and set the rest of the slice on the napkin. Was there someone—someone special—she didn't want to hear the gossip? "Maybe you'd like to explain that."

She stared at her hands for a moment before looking up, meeting his gaze. "I guess it's going to come out anyway… I have a daughter. Her name's Fiona."

"Oh…huh." Well, that explained who Fiona was. But…Meg was a mother? He hadn't seen that coming. He recalled Meg as a little girl with that mass of red hair, freckles and those beautiful eyes. Did her daughter look like her? His throat tightened with longing for something he couldn't—or wouldn't—name. He'd made his choice six years ago and now he had no right to any possessiveness or room for regrets.

After Meg's first letter, he'd received orders to report to a marine expeditionary unit and spent months deep in Afghanistan's desolate countryside. Due to a snafu, he hadn't received the rest of her letters until getting back to a forward operating base. Someone had bundled the letters as if preparing to return them. Before he could open them, fate had intervened in the form of an IED, killing and maiming his fellow marines, and he'd decided to set Meg free without ever reading the letters, afraid he'd change his mind if he did.

"Are you and the child's father still—" he cleared his throat before continuing "—involved?"

Chapter Three

"No, he hasn't been a part of our lives for a long time." Meg chewed on a pepperoni slice she'd picked off her pizza, but had trouble swallowing past the tightness in her throat. He didn't even ask if he was Fiona's father. Evidently, the thought never occurred to him. If he'd asked, hopped up on asthma meds or not, she would've confessed. But he hadn't. She picked another pepperoni off the pizza but put it back. They were her favorite part, but that last one had tasted like cardboard. *No, Meg, that was the lie you've been telling.*

"Do you have a picture?" When he opened the soda, the tab snapped off and he tossed it aside.

Digging into her pocket, Meg pulled out her cell phone and thumbed through her photos. She found one her dad had sent a few days ago: a wide shot another tourist must've taken. It was a smiling Fiona standing between Mac and Doris in front of the Grand Canyon. The photo was close enough to see Fiona but not so close as to show her facial features clearly…especially her gray eyes. Riley's eyes.

Her heart pounding, she handed him the phone. And this was a picture. What would she do when Fiona arrived in person? She was simultaneously too tired and wired from the asthma meds to think about that now.

Riley stared at the screen, a slight frown puckering his brow. Using his thumb and index finger he enlarged the image, and Meg's fingers clenched against the urge to snatch the phone back. What was he thinking? Could he see himself like she did each time she looked at her precious daughter? Sure, everyone said Fiona looked like her, but Meg saw Riley in everything Fiona did or said.

Finally, he lifted his head and handed the phone back; an expression that looked a lot like longing crossed his face. But that was crazy. He'd chosen the marines over settling down. Did he now regret it? She pushed those dangerous thoughts aside.

"Except for the glasses, she looks just like you."

Her short laugh was a mixture of relief and regret. "Liam says it's like growing up with me all over again."

Laughing, he shook his head. "I can't imagine Liam as an uncle."

"Yeah, and Fiona loves it when he babysits because she has him wrapped around her little finger."

"You let Liam babysit?"

She stiffened for a moment but his lopsided grin proved he was teasing. "*Pfft*, yeah, he fools us sometimes by acting like a responsible adult."

"Huh… Liam babysitting his niece… I *have* been

gone a long time." One side of his mouth lifted in a half smile.

"He's twenty-nine, same as you." She licked her bottom lip. "And you're a responsible adult... Haven't you ever thought about settling down?"

His brows drew together. "I am settled, Meg."

"I see." But did she?

You have a blind spot when it comes to that boy, her ma used to say. If her ma could see Riley now, she'd see he was no longer a boy. No, the boy Meg had fallen in love with was a man.

"What about your parents? How are they?"

"Mom's in Seattle with husband number three and Dad's in Boca Raton dating women my age."

"How come you didn't go to stay with one of them?" She and Fiona might have moved out of her dad's house, but she couldn't imagine not having him or her brother in their lives.

"We do better with a buffer of half a country between us."

"But your mother, she—"

He shook his head. "She spent my childhood trying to prevent me from having any kind of relationship with my dad."

Instead of eating the pizza slice in her hand, she laid it on the napkin. "Maybe she thought she was protecting you."

He released a noisy puff of air. "Short of abuse, there's no excuse for keeping a child from his or her father."

She pushed her pizza to the side. "I'm sorry. I didn't mean to make you spend money on the pizza then not eat it, but I'm exhausted. I... I just want to lie down."

He pushed his chair back and rose. "Do you want me to turn the television and lights off so you can sleep?"

"No, that's okay. No matter how exhausted I am, the meds key me up so it's hard to sleep. I'll lie down and read for a bit. That might help."

He snagged another slice of pizza and ate it standing up. "If you're done in the bathroom, I'll take a shower. If you need anything, give me a shout."

She settled on the bed with her e-reader, but she couldn't concentrate on the words in front of her. *Short of abuse, there's no excuse for keeping a child from his or her father.* Riley's words haunted her.

Riley tugged a pair of tattered jeans on over his black boxer briefs and pulled on a faded gray T-shirt to cover his scars. Brushing his teeth, he thought about Meg asking him if he'd thought about settling down. What had she been asking him? When he'd looked at the picture of Meg's little girl, something had curled around his heart; a feeling he couldn't shake. After his parents' disastrous marriage, he'd decided not making that commitment in the first place seemed the wisest option. Of course, Meg would see things differently because her parents had provided her with a stable and loving home. He couldn't risk what he felt for Meg turning into a morass of bitterness like his parents. He assumed they loved one another at some point but it must've been before he was born.

Maybe if he explained why he was content to let the marines be his family, Meg would understand. He hated hurting her and decided he'd give explaining a shot, but he opened the bathroom door to find Meg sound asleep. She was on top of the covers, an e-reader in her lap, her head at an uncomfortable-looking angle against the headboard. Damn, he couldn't leave her like that. Dropping his dirty clothes on top of his canvas pack, he went to her.

He laid the reading device on the nightstand bolted to the wall and lifted her legs while pulling the covers back with his other hand. After he'd gotten them pushed aside, he settled her on the bed, surprised she didn't wake up, but she just murmured something and snuggled up to the stuffed bear. Maybe the medications had wiped her out after all. He rearranged the covers and tucked her in, wishing for a moment he was that stuffed toy.

Leaning over the bed, he pressed his mouth to her forehead in a light kiss, inhaling her fresh, soapy scent. He brushed a stray curl off her cheek and tucked it behind her ear. Shaking his head at his actions, he turned off the light, stripped out of his jeans and T-shirt and crawled into the other bed. Lacing his fingers together, he rested his head on his hands and stared at the ceiling. His first week in Afghanistan, Riley had expected Liam and Mac to show up, looking to castrate him for seducing Meggie. Not that anything they could have done to him would have been any worse than what he'd done to himself. How many nights had he lain awake in some hellhole, torturing himself with thoughts of her?

Meg jerked awake and sat up. Where was she? Her mind played back the events of the evening. Riley. The ER. Then the motel. She'd woken earlier, hot and sweaty, so she'd removed her robe, but fatigue had dragged her back to sleep.

The noise again.

It was coming from the other bed. Riley? Meg got up and went to the bathroom to turn on that light rather than the ones in the room. If he was having a nightmare, she didn't want to startle him.

Riley thrashed on the bed, the covers tangled around his feet. Was he reliving some battlefield trauma? Or standard nightmare fare?

"Riley?" She took a few cautious steps toward the bed and spoke a little louder. "Riley?"

He jackknifed upright in the bed and glanced in her direction, but his expression held no hint of recognition. He drew in several ragged breaths, scrubbing his fingers over his face and in his hair. Swinging his legs over the side of the bed, he bowed his head and rested his arms between his knees.

Meg used the light spilling from the bathroom to observe him. His black boxer briefs hugged his hips and thighs, dipping lower in the back as he sat on the mattress and reminding her how he'd felt under her hands, how she'd spent years closing her eyes and remembering. Now, here he was, alone with her in the dark, awake and tormented, and she wanted to comfort him, wanted him to comfort her, wanted the years and the space between them to melt away. But that was a childish wish. Still… "Riley?"

He lifted his head and his jaw dropped. "Meggie?"

"I… I…"

"Why aren't you in bed?" Jumping up, he took a stumbling step toward her. "Are you okay? Is something wrong?"

"I'm fine." She shook her head. "I… You…"

He took her arm and nudged her to the edge of the bed, pressing on her shoulders till she sat. "Are you sure you're okay?"

"I'm fine. You were having a nightmare." Her stomach twisted at Riley's suffering. She yearned to kiss him, tell him how much she admired his courage. Would he welcome the attention or reject her?

He sank down next to her, causing the mattress to dip. "Sorry if I woke you."

Meg touched his thigh, and when she would have pulled away, he covered her hand with his callused one.

Her breath stuttered in her chest. "Do you get a lot of nightmares?"

"Not really." He threaded his fingers through hers.

She stifled the urge to throw her arms around him and hang on for dear life. That would be a big mistake. A whopper. "Was this one about your time in Afghanistan?"

He squeezed her hand. "I don't remember. Just a crazy dream."

"Sometimes it helps to talk it out." She kept her tone neutral despite her pounding heart.

He glanced down at their entwined hands, dropping hers as if it had scorched his. "I told you, I don't remember."

She stiffened at his icy tone and shifted her body away from his. This time the tightness in her lungs had nothing to do with asthma.

He jumped off the bed and pulled his pants on. "I'm sorry I woke you. You need your sleep."

He grabbed his shirt off the floor and yanked it over his head. Stuffing his bare feet into his boots, he said, "I need some air. You should get your rest."

"Where are you going?"

His hand flexed around the doorknob. "I'll be right outside if you need anything."

"Do...do you want me to come?" She remembered

those bottles of whiskey and her stomach sank. Is that why he needed them? Maybe if she could get him to talk, he wouldn't need the alcohol.

He spoke to her from the open door. "I can look after myself, Meghan. I've been doing it for quite some time now."

Pain squeezed her chest, leaving her feeling vulnerable, confused. "Fine."

The door clicking shut behind him was his response.

Riley leaned against his truck, lifting one foot to rest against the driver's door. Those nightmares left him raw and aching to escape his own skin, reminding him how, as a kid, he'd longed to escape those vicious arguments between his parents. As a young boy he'd been convinced if he'd been better, stronger, smarter, he could've solved his parents' marital problems, make them a whole family once again. The nightmares proved escape was an illusion.

He let himself back into the room. He'd stayed close so he'd be able to hear her if she began coughing too much. The light still shone from the bathroom and he could see Meg huddled under the covers. He toed off his untied boots and went to her. The light from the bathroom lit her face and highlighted tracks in her cheeks. Had he caused those tears? He skimmed the tips of his fingers across her smooth skin, and his chest squeezed so tight it was a wonder it didn't crush his heart.

He'd hurt her, but what else could he have done once he'd become aware she'd removed the robe and sat next to him in nothing but a tank top and skimpy sleep shorts? His body had reacted immediately and noticeably, so he'd had to get out of there. Quick. Or be embarrassed like a horny teenager. He knew the fastest and best way to do that had been to reject her touch, her concern…her. It had killed him to do it, but what choice did he have? If he'd stayed, he'd have leaned into her touch and done a heck of a lot more than kiss her forehead. He had to keep reminding himself she was still recovering from a life-threatening asthma attack.

And she was still off-limits. Liam had made that clear the last time he'd called him. *I understand getting your rocks off before leaving, but I never suspected it would be with my sister. I never thought you'd take advantage of that crush, or that you'd screw her as a going-away present.* The morning after their night of passion, Meg had pleaded with Riley not to tell Liam and he'd agreed. Obviously, she'd come clean to her brother at some point.

Riley gave up trying to sleep around dawn, rolled out of bed, threw his clothes on and slipped out of the room. Big-box home improvement stores catering to general contractors opened early, so he'd take advantage of that and pick up some supplies for Meg's basement. Before he left Loon Lake, her cellar would be free of mold and as flood proof as possible.

On the way back to the motel, he went through the burger joint's drive-through and picked up two coffees. He juggled his half-empty cup and her full one as he entered the room.

Meg was just coming out of the bathroom, dressed in faded jeans that hugged her slender curves and an oversize white cotton button-down shirt, the tails tied at the waist. She had her flyaway curls pulled back from her face in a messy ponytail and the color was back in her cheeks.

His tongue stuck to the roof of his mouth as he stood

and drank in her girl-next-door appearance. *This*. This was the picture he'd carry back with him and pull out on long, lonely nights when it was just him and his M16. "I...uh, bought coffee."

"I see that." She set the small bundle of clothes in her hands on the bed and crossed the room.

She stood before him, looking more beautiful than he'd remembered from that night almost six years ago. Her color was back and a smattering of freckles danced across the bridge of her nose and the top of her cheeks, as well. That night he'd rolled his tongue over them, savoring her sweetness.

"Riley?"

"Sorry." He shoved the coffee at her and reached into his pocket to toss some sugar packets, napkins and creamers on the table.

He peeled the lid off his coffee. "Since you didn't eat much of last night's pizza, I thought you might like a proper breakfast. Is that restaurant on the town square still open?"

"Aunt Polly's? Yeah, it's still there." She set her cup on the table, then picked up several packets and shook them down before ripping off one end.

When she bent her head over her task, he leaned closer, his fingers itching to pluck a curl from its confinement. He shoved his free hand into his pocket and jingled the loose change. "They still serve buckwheat pancakes with boysenberry syrup?"

She looked up and nodded, swallowing hard, the muscles in her slender neck working.

He gulped his coffee, despite its lingering heat stinging his tongue. The empty to-go cup collapsed in his hand and he tossed it on the table. "I'm taking you there for breakfast."

Her eyes widened then narrowed. "Are you asking me or telling me?"

Incapable of keeping his hands off her, he clumsily brushed a stray curl off her forehead. "Which do you prefer?"

She frowned but didn't pull away from his touch. "Asking would be nice."

"Then consider yourself asked. I've been craving… pancakes."

Something flickered in her eyes, but she blinked and it disappeared. "Well, in that case, I'll get my stuff packed up. It's not much so it won't take but a minute."

He flexed his fingers. "Good. I'm…starved."

Coffee sloshed over the cup onto her hand and she grimaced.

"Here." He took her cup and handed her a napkin since licking the coffee from her fingers wasn't a viable option.

"Thanks." She wiped her hand. "You must've been up early."

"I went to the home improvement store," he answered automatically and mentally kicked himself. What if she still wanted to fight him on this? "I'll take a look at your basement. Clean up what I can to be sure there's no lingering mold and see about sealing the cement against further water incursion."

She sucked on her lower lip as she seemed to be considering his offer. "Thanks. I appreciate the help."

They drove toward Loon Lake on the four-lane highway maintained by the state. He smiled to himself at the signs warning of moose crossings. At least the dangers here were posted, unlike the roads in Afghanistan, where a roadside bomb could change your life in an instant. Although he guessed hitting a moose at high speed would accomplish the same thing.

As they entered the town, he slowed to admire the tidy, brick-fronted businesses that sported bright-colored awnings, American flags and wooden buckets containing flowers. He tightened his grip on the steering wheel. Those decorative buckets would be the perfect place to conceal an explosive device.

"Riley?"

Had she sensed the change in him? To break the spell and avoid questions, he pointed to a place with tables on the sidewalk. "That looks new."

"Yes, that's a microbrewery. It's quite popular on the weekends."

"Beer?"

"Hard cider." Meg waved at a woman sweeping the sidewalk in front a bookstore next to the brewery.

He slowed the truck again as they drove past a café with a red awning that declared Aunt Polly's in white lettering. He didn't have to go too far past to park and pulled into the angled parking spot.

Jumping out, he rushed to help Meg before feeding coins into the parking meter.

His fingers twitched, but he refrained from touching her as they walked the short distance to the café, respecting her concerns over gossip. They entered the bustling restaurant and warm air carried the scents of coffee, cinnamon and bacon grease. Directly across from the entrance was a long counter with half a dozen stools filled with customers, booths lined up along the front windows and a couple of unoccupied tables between the counter and the booths. Riley noticed that everyone smiled, nodded or waved at Meg.

"Meg, long time no see." A stout blonde with a glass coffeepot in one hand and a white cloth in the other greeted them and inclined her head at a vacant booth. "Have a seat and I'll be right with you."

The blonde waitress, Trudi, according to her name tag, came over soon after they'd slipped into the red vinyl booth. She put two pebbled plastic tumblers with ice water on the table along with dog-eared menus. She flashed a smile at Riley. "Riley Cooper, as I live and breathe, it is you."

Meg rolled her eyes. "Told you news travels fast."

He chuckled. "I never doubted you."

"Are you staying at the Coopers' old place?"

"That's where I'm staying, but it doesn't belong to us anymore." Riley opened his menu.

"True, but it will be the Coopers' old place until the new owners sell. Then it will be the Duffys' old place," the waitress explained.

Riley winked at the waitress and turned his attention to Meg. "So, Meg, does that mean you live in your old house?"

Meg glanced heavenward. "Yeah, despite owning it, I live in Dad's old house."

Riley tapped her arm with his menu. "Just think, when you move, the new people will live in Meg's old place."

Meg rolled her eyes. "This is starting to sound too much like 'who's on first,' if you want my opinion."

A man in blue overalls seated at the counter held up a coffee mug and pointed it at the waitress, who grumbled, "Hold your horses, Ralph. Can't you see I'm waiting on someone?"

"All I see is you jawing with the newcomer everyone at the Pic-N-Save is so fired up about," the customer shot back.

The waitress shook her head. "Don't pay him no mind. What can I get you to drink?"

Riley ordered another coffee and Meg ordered juice. Silence fell over their booth when the waitress hustled off to fill their drink orders.

"I—"

"Are you—"

Riley chuckled. "Ladies first."

"Were you serious when you told Kevin he could help with my basement cleanup?" She unwrapped her straw and stuck it in her water glass.

"Of course." Evidently, his answer pleased her because her eyes lit up. He shouldn't be surprised at her willingness to help one of her students. Her parents had led by example. So had his, but with vastly different results.

"Thank you." She sipped her water and fiddled with the wrapper from her straw.

"My helping him out pleases you?"

"He's a good kid. Life hasn't given him a lot of breaks. It's sweet of you to step up and help him."

The waitress returned with coffee, juice and a cheerful grin before he could respond, but he was enjoying basking in the glow of Meg's smile. Him, sweet? Nah, but he was glad to help the kid out and earn Meg's gratitude as a bonus.

Trudi pulled her order pad and pencil out of the pocket in her apron. "Decide what you'd like?"

More of Meg's smiles, please.

Meg must've ordered because the chirpy waitress was looking expectantly at him. Heat rose in his face. Jeez, he was worse than a teen with his first crush. "Buckwheat pancakes, and do you have boysenberry syrup?"

Meg and Trudi exchanged looks.

Riley's glance shifted between the two women. "What?"

"Flatlander," they replied in unison and grinned.

"Hey, technically Meg is, too," he pointed out. He knew flatlander was a term locals ascribed to people not born and raised in Vermont.

"Yeah, but she doesn't advertise it by refusing maple syrup." The waitress scooped up the menus and scurried off, shaking her head and chuckling.

Unable to keep from touching Meg any longer, he reached across the table and traced his fingertip over the top of her hand. "So, you're teaching at the high school level now? You used to say you wanted to teach the lower grades."

She glanced at his hand on hers but didn't pull away. "I thought that's what I wanted, too, but after subbing at the high school, I changed my focus to secondary education. I liked the extra challenge."

"So, are you teaching full-time or subbing? I didn't think school was out for the summer yet." Although the marines had given him the sense of family he'd craved as a child, he felt a twinge of disappointment at missing all the changes in Meg's life. He hated having to ask the most basic questions about her life.

"It's not, but I'm subbing when I can." She sipped her water. "Finishing school was put on the back burner for a while when I had Fiona, then Ma was sick, and well..."

"And now?" His hand clasped over hers.

"Now everything is back on track. I got my degree earlier this month." She met his gaze. "I'm a part of the community here and have applied for a teaching job at the high school."

"You always did want to become a teacher."

She lifted one shoulder in a shrug. "I can't explain it, but from the moment I walked into that classroom in kindergarten and saw that teacher, I knew that's what I wanted to do."

He squeezed her hand. "I remember you were always playing school as a kid."

"Yeah, I had the smartest stuffed animals on the block."

He laughed, glad Meg had found her place in the world, and yet an indefinable sadness thickened his throat. Would he have been part of the good life she'd made if he hadn't chosen the marines over her? His hand tightened over hers on the table. Coming home each night to Meg and the little red-haired girl with pink glasses held a certain appeal.

His chest tightened as he tried to imagine himself reading a story and tucking Meg's daughter into bed each night. Did little girls enjoy tossing a ball around in the yard? He doubted she'd be interested in learning to identify incoming artillery rounds by their sound.

The waitress appeared beside their booth and Meg pulled her hand free as their server lowered the plates. "Buckwheat pancakes and boysenberry syrup. There's different grades of, *ahem*, real syrup on the end of the booth in case you come to your senses. Can I get you anything else? More juice? Coffee?"

"I'm good." Meg smiled at the waitress.

His mind still on Meg and her daughter, he had to

clear his clogged throat. That's what he got for mourning the loss of something he'd never had. "Me, too, thanks."

They fell silent as they buttered their pancakes and poured syrup over the stacks. He took a few bites and smiled at the flavors he'd remembered. "Mmm, just like I remembered."

She looked up from her breakfast and smiled. "It's comforting to know some things remain the same."

He could plan a future around that smile. "Coming home after a deployment to see all the changes is a reminder that life goes on without us."

"Is that good or bad?" She wiped her mouth with a napkin.

"A little of both, I guess." He rubbed his chest. Meg's life had gone on without him.

"I know you're a marine, but what exactly do you do?"

"I'm part of a marine expeditionary unit," he said, pride evident in his tone. He'd worked his butt off in training.

"Oh, wow." Her eyes widened. "What do they do?"

"We go ahead of everyone else and make sure it's safe." He shrugged, but her interest pleased him.

"That sounds…" She dropped her fork and reached toward him, but her hand stalled in the middle of the table. "That sounds…scary."

Oh, man, he wanted her proud, not frightened. He set his white ceramic mug down and took her hand. "We're highly trained and very well equipped."

"I know but—"

"Can I get you folks anything else?" The waitress paused alongside their booth.

He looked to Meg but she shook her head and he

dropped her hand. "No, we're good. Just the check, please, ma'am."

"Oh, hon." The waitress smiled and winked. "It's already taken care of."

"It is?" Once again he glanced at Meg, but she gave him an *I have no idea* shrug.

"Anonymously. We may be a peace loving bunch, but we still appreciate your service, hon," she said with a wave of her hand and moved on to the next booth.

"At least I can leave her a good tip." He shifted and pulled out his wallet, noticing the slip of paper he'd gotten during his mandated evaluation after deployment. It had the name of the veterans' support group nearest to Loon Lake. He stood, tossed some bills on the table, folded his wallet and stuffed it into his pocket. Maybe if he was staying he'd see if he could offer to help others not as lucky as himself...but he was leaving.

Still, he couldn't help wonder what it would be like to come to this restaurant on weekends with Meg and her little girl or to have them waiting for him with the other welcoming families at the end of a tour. After his first deployment, he'd searched the gathered crowd for a familiar face, his seabag weighing him down as he trudged through the happy crowd. His parents had both contacted him, separately of course, with apologies for not being able to meet him. But he hadn't been searching for his parents. It was Meg. Always Meg.

Chapter Four

Meg stood at the top of the stairs where the murmur of voices along with a strong chemical odor drifted up from the basement. She was torn between being grateful for Riley's help and feeling guilty. She didn't want him to think she was using him. And would he regret helping her once he found out about Fiona? This was the second day in a row Riley and Kevin, who came after his school day ended, had worked down there, first cleaning and now, according to Riley, they were waterproofing the cinder block foundation. Her guess was the paint they were using was responsible for the strong smell.

"Kevin? Will you stay and have supper with us?" Was she inviting Kevin because she was concerned about him? Or was she using his presence as a buffer?

Riley appeared at the bottom of the stairs, hands on hips, a white mask hanging around his neck. "What are you doing? You're supposed to be outside while we do this."

"I have been," she shot back, but his concern curled around her heart and took the heat out of her words. "I was going to put some burgers on the grill and needed to know how many. And why isn't that face mask on? It doesn't do any good dangling around your neck. Kevin? You'd better be wearing yours."

A muffled "yes, ma'am" answered her question, but Kevin remained out of sight.

"Is that a yes on staying to supper, too?" She was being polite, not arranging a chaperone or another excuse not to come clean about Fiona.

She heard Kevin's voice but couldn't make out what he was saying. Riley made a shooing motion at her when she leaned down, then turned his head presumably toward Kevin.

Riley turned back to her. "He's staying."

A muffled protest and Riley shook his head. "He's staying."

They'd gone through much the same thing yesterday when Kevin kept insisting he didn't want to impose. But Meg caught the look of longing on the teen's face as he glanced at the supper she'd prepared. Riley had seen it, too, because he clamped an arm around Kevin's shoulders and insisted he stay. Riley's simple kindness toward the boy warmed Meg. *He'd be a good father.* The thought twirled around in her head as she waited for a perfect moment to tell him about Fiona. *That would have been five years ago, Meg. But you were too busy nursing your wounded pride.* Guilt sat on her stomach like a boulder, getting heavier each day that went by without telling him.

But after spending a childhood and puberty embarrassing herself by wearing her heart on her sleeve, she'd reached the breaking point when that large manila envelope arrived with all her unopened letters.

She'd gotten over her pride and screwed up her courage last night, but Kevin had some car trouble and she'd dozed off in the Adirondack chair on her porch by the time they'd gotten the car started. She'd woken up, but Riley had insisted she go in and go to bed.

"Meg?"

Riley's voice broke into her thoughts, yanking her back to the present and scattering the image of him joining her in bed. "Huh?"

He lifted his eyebrow. "Fresh air. Now."

She glowered at him. "Face mask in place. Now."

Riley's soft chuckle followed her and raised goose bumps on the back of her neck as she gathered up the tray with the ingredients for supper and went outside.

Meg locked her front door and pocketed the key. Most year-round residents of Loon Lake only locked their doors during the height of tourist season. Growing up, she'd spent summers and school holidays here and the rest of her time in Boston, so locking doors was a habit she couldn't shake. She glanced across the yard. No sign of Riley's truck. Wherever he'd gone, he'd left early. She hated to admit it, but looking out her window was one of the first things she'd done the past two mornings since Riley had finished work in her basement.

He could come and go as he pleased. She had no hold over him. Ah, but would she once she told him about Fiona? As much as she coveted the idea of having him in her life, she wasn't sure how she'd be able to handle having that permanent tie if—no, *when*, since she needed to stay grounded in reality—he had another woman in his life. It had become easy to turn to him, depend on him, during the past two days. He wouldn't appreciate having her cling once he decided he needed to move on. And Riley was way too sexy not to attract the interest of countless women. Lord only knew how many he might have been involved with since their night together. Just because she'd chosen not to be in a relationship didn't mean he felt the same.

She had a life of her own, and as if to prove it, she'd decided not to call him this morning to ask for a ride. Well, yeah, she'd waited until the last moment to leave in case he returned, but that didn't prove anything.

A black pickup pulled into the shared driveway as she stepped off her porch. She pursed her lips, annoyed with the way her heart sped up at the sight of Riley jumping out of his truck.

"Where are you headed to?"

"I was going to—" The rest of her response was lost in a fit of coughing. She pulled the inhaler from her pocket and puffed twice.

"I knew I shouldn't have let you stay home while we waterproofed your basement." He moved closer. "Do I need to take you to—"

"No, I don't need a doctor. Or a motel. You and Kevin did a great job ventilating the place." She pocketed the inhaler. "The coughing always lingers for a while. I'm capable of walking a mile and besides, I am taking my meds even if they make me jittery."

"So where were you going?" He stopped in front of her and planted his feet shoulder width apart. Today he wore jeans and a gray T-shirt that showcased his broad shoulders, the faded red lettering declaring United States Marine.

She rubbed her hand across her chin, hoping she hadn't literally just drooled. "I was headed into town."

He raised his brow. "Walking?"

God, she wanted to throw her arms around him, maybe lean against that rock-hard chest again. She shuffled her feet, kicking at the loose rocks in the gravel driveway. "It's less than a mile."

He tilted his head toward the road beyond the tree line. "But there aren't any sidewalks and that's a main road. The cars come fast around those corners. Why didn't you ask me for a ride?"

Okay, it was obvious he saw her not as some sexy woman, but more like one of those poor, unfortunate victims with a wasting disease in a Jane Austen novel. The women relegated to secondary roles due to ill health. "Well, for one thing, you weren't here—"

"I gave you my cell number."

And calling him to ask for a ride would've cemented her role, not as a capable woman, but as someone who needed rescuing. "And I'm perfectly capable of getting into town by myself."

"I worry about you walking into town."

She ground her back teeth. How dare he treat her as an invalid! She'd looked after herself before he arrived and she'd do it again after he left. "And I appreciate your concern, but I'm not some project you need to take on while you're here. I'm quite adept at taking care of myself." No, she wanted him to see her as an adult, not that child who used to tag along when they were kids.

He shook his head. "I didn't mean it like that."

"Then what *did* you mean?"

"I understand you don't *need* my help...but I still want to offer it. And...and I'd like it if you'd accept it." He drew his lower lip between his teeth as he watched her.

"Fair enough." And it wasn't as if she wasn't grateful for his help or such a martyr that she wouldn't accept it. "You can give me a ride."

He smiled smugly and swept his arm in an encompassing arc toward his truck. "Where in town are you going?"

"The church on the green." She fell into step beside him, enjoying the clean scent of his soap and what she suspected was fabric softener.

He opened the passenger door and waited while she climbed in. "Church on a Thursday morning?"

She nodded. "When I'm not working, I volunteer at a weekly luncheon where everyone is welcome, regardless of ability to pay. Some people use it as an excuse to socialize and make generous donations to keep us afloat, and some come because it's their only decent meal, so there's a mix of people. I think the pastor uses it to keep an eye out for people who might need a little extra assistance."

Riley made sure she was settled before shutting the door. Truth was, although he did worry about Meg walking along the highway, spending more time with her had been his main goal.

"So you volunteer?" He checked for traffic before pulling onto the highway.

"Yeah, I like to give back to the community."

He slowed for a flagman in front of a road crew trimming trees and glanced at her. Sounded like Meg had integrated into life at Loon Lake and she was a vital and active member of the community.

Loon Lake was what Riley thought of as one of those quintessential New England towns photographed and featured on decorative calendars. The kind where businesses and homes huddled around a town green complete with a gazebo that doubled as a bandstand.

A large white clapboard church with black shutters and a giant steeple anchored the green at one end. He pulled into the gravel lot next to the church. Even though the building dated back to the Revolutionary War, it appeared well-maintained. "Where do you want me to drop you off?"

"You're not coming in?" Her tone indicated surprise and maybe confusion.

He slowed near the steps leading to the giant double doors. "I figured you wouldn't want me there…gossip and all."

She shrugged. "You showing up here won't increase or decrease the gossip. Besides, you can keep Ogle company."

"Ogle Whatley? The old guy who used to own the garage?" Regret knotted in his belly. Why had he cut himself off from all these wonderful people? His childhood memories weren't all bad and yet he'd locked them away as if letting one out would mean the rest could come spilling out.

"He still owns it. Runs it with his grandson."

He shook his head and grinned. "He must be a hundred by now."

"I'm sure he'd appreciate hearing that." Meg laughed. "I swear he looks the same as he did when I was five, and I thought he was ancient then."

"Don't tell me Ogle volunteers, too."

"Yeah, he likes to keep tabs on our vets. We have a few that come on a regular basis. Some from the Korean War are widowed and get lonesome or tired of their own cooking. The older guys also come to talk with the younger ones back from Afghanistan who might be having a tough time adjusting. Ogle is very good at getting them to talk." Meg gave him an expectant glance. "So, you'll come in?"

"Not sure how much help I can be, but I'll give it a shot."

"Great. They'll be setting up in the basement, so pull around to the back."

"Basement?"

She blew out a noisy breath. "Oh, for heaven's sakes, I'm fine and there's no mold in the church basement."

"Do you have your inhaler?" Riley asked as he pulled the truck around to the rear parking lot.

"Yes, I do. Oh, look, there's Ogle."

A rotund bald man was getting out of a restored bright red 1949 Mercury M47 pickup. Riley gave a low whistle. "That truck is a work of art."

"Yeah, he's pretty proud of it."

"As he should be." Riley parked next to the antique truck.

Ogle sauntered over and gave Meg a hug when she got out of Riley's truck.

Riley came around and shook hands with the older man. "Sir."

"Riley Cooper, how be ya?" Ogle clapped him on the shoulder before releasing his hand. "Heard you was back."

"News travels fast around here." Riley's gaze shifted to Meg, but she was all smiles.

"And the fact that Jan the nurse from the ER is his daughter-in-law doesn't hurt." Meg punched Ogle on the arm.

"*Bah*, Meggie," Ogle scolded. "I didn't hear it from Jan. Folks down at the Pic-N-Save was jawing about some new guy in town and Tavie got wind of it. That old woman wouldn't rest till she got to the bottom of it."

Riley tucked his sunglasses around the neck of his T-shirt and frowned. Why did he think he could slip into town unnoticed for thirty days? He should've realized his return would stir up interest, but then he'd planned on sitting alone in his cottage. "I'm just here for some R&R before getting back to my men."

Ogle shifted the toothpick in his mouth to the other side and glanced at Meg before turning his attention back to Riley. "Sorry you ain't sticking around. Hear you've been doing a lot to help Meg here."

Meg cleared her throat. "I'd better get inside. They'll be wondering where I am."

Ogle hooked his thumbs in the suspenders of his overalls and laughed. "You'll have to do double duty today without Miss Fiona."

Meg shook her head but smiled good-naturedly. "I have a feeling things will get done a bit quicker today."

"But everyone will be missin' that little ray of sunshine," Ogle said as Riley fell into step beside him to follow Meg into the church.

And just like that, Riley felt like an outsider in Meg's life. It saddened him to think about her having a daughter, a vital part of her that he'd never even met. As he helped Ogle set up folding tables in the large, open basement of the church, he watched Meg working and chatting with the other women. A woman asked Meg a question and Meg looked as though she was giving her instructions. Meg had carved out a whole life for herself and, as before, he was on the outside looking in. Despite all the time spent with the McBrides, he'd never been one of them. But that was on him because they'd welcomed him.

"Sergeant Cooper?"

After pushing a metal folding chair into place at a rectangular table, Riley turned in the direction of the unfamiliar voice. "Yes?"

"You helping us out today?" A kid not much older than Kevin, his hands jammed into the pockets of raggedy jeans, his shoulders slouched, was intently watching him.

"Yeah, I thought I'd hang around and help out." Why wasn't the kid in school? "Have we met?"

"Nah, but I'm a friend of Kevin's and he told me about how you let him help out."

Ogle sauntered up and put his hand on the boy's shoulder. "Danny, son, you should introduce yourself. Sergeant Cooper doesn't know you."

"Oh, uh, you're right, Mr. Ogle." The kid blushed and ducked his head but held out a hand. "Danny Simmons. Nice to meet you, Sergeant Cooper."

"Pleasure to meet you, Danny." Riley shook his hand and glanced across the basement to Meg working and chatting with the other women in the kitchen. He admired the woman she'd become.

"Danny, son, why don't you get some more chairs from the closet?" Ogle said.

Once the teen was out of earshot, Ogle leaned over

to Riley. "We've been trying to get him back in school but…"

Riley recalled when, during one of the more stressful times between his parents, he'd thought about quitting school, if just to get their attention. Thankfully, Mac McBride had talked some sense into him.

Ogle watched Danny trot off to fetch more chairs. "He's good friends with Kevin and we hoped Kevin getting his life back on track would help, but so far, nada. Not for lack of trying on our Meggie's part."

"Oh?"

"Our Meggie has a tender heart. Hate to see her get it broken," Ogle remarked and stuck a toothpick in his mouth.

Riley nodded. Yep, Ogle's message came through loud and clear.

Danny came back pushing a hand truck loaded with more folding chairs.

Ogle had wandered off and Riley was alone with the kid.

Danny set up a chair. "So, you're like a marine."

"That's right."

"You must be the one Ms. McBride talked about."

Riley pulled another chair off the stack. "Oh?"

"Yeah. She's always telling me stuff." Danny leaned against the chair he'd just unfolded. "When I told her I was thinking of joining up, she said she knew a marine… and sounded like…all proud and stuff. Must be nice to have someone be proud of you, ya know?"

Meg had used him as an example? Riley glanced across the room to the kitchen, searching for her. She looked up from what she'd been doing and their gazes met. Although her brows drew together in a puzzled frown, she smiled and he returned it. Someone spoke to her and she turned to them, but not before giving one last little smile just for him.

Riley turned his attention back to Danny. "You'd have to finish high school or at least get your GED."

"That's what she said." The kid cleared his throat. "You get lots of respect for being a marine, yeah?"

"It's not the uniform, Danny, but the man wearing it."

The church basement began to fill up with people, chatting and laughing. Riley was going to wait until the others had been served to be sure there was enough, but noticed Danny following his example. The kid looked like he could use a decent meal so Riley suggested they get in line. When Meg saw him with Danny, she gave him a special smile along with lunch.

After lunch, Ogle crossed the room to talk with a man clutching a desert camo boonie hat between his hands. He looked to be about Riley's age. Was that one of the Afghanistan vets Meg had mentioned? Riley recognized that self-contained pose. As though if he allowed himself to relax he might fly apart.

Riley turned to Danny. "Who is that with Ogle?"

"That's Travis. He's ex-army."

Riley wandered over and listened as Ogle spoke about some of his experiences in Vietnam.

"Haunts me to this day… Khe Sanh…twenty-fifth of February, nineteen sixty-eight." Ogle hooked his thumbs under the bib of his overalls and squeezed as if needing to hang on to something. "My squad was one of two wiped out… Only survived because while them NVA were executing wounded, I…"

Three school-age children clattered down the steps of the church basement. Without warning, Riley was back in a dusty school building in Kandahar, cradling his M4 and sweating under his IMT Vest—

"Riley?" Meg's voice snapped him back to the present and he blinked several times.

Ogle stared at him with a sympathetic *been there, done that* expression, but Meggie's face… Oh, God, the color had leached from her face. Fear. He could smell it. No, wait, that was him…he was soaked in sweat.

Riley lifted his arm and swiped his shirtsleeve across his forehead.

"You okay?" Meg peered at him, her face etched in concern.

"Fine…just felt a bit warm." He wasn't about to go into details and scare her even more.

She shifted, looking uncertain. "If…if you'd rather leave now, I can catch a ride."

Great. Had he scared her that much? "I brought you. I'll take you home. I'm going to talk to Travis for a bit, so take your time."

"Oh…okay." She touched his arm. "I'm almost done."

Ogle had been silent during the short exchange with Meg, but he cleared his throat and patted Riley's shoulder. "Son, if you ever need someone to, uh, you know, uh, make sense of some of this…"

Riley nodded, but he was alive and so many of his fellow marines were dead. Where was the sense in that? None. But he had to at least try.

He stuck his hand out to Travis. "Got a sec?"

Meg walked toward Riley's truck, her mind spinning, her stomach churning. She'd loved Riley since realizing there was more to boys than cooties; she'd succeeded in seducing him at nineteen and had a child with him.

Acid burned her stomach to realize she didn't know *this* Riley. She'd known the boy who'd helped her catch frogs, the teenager who'd awkwardly held her when her dad wouldn't let her get a dog because of her asthma and the young man who'd made love to her that night, the night they'd made a baby. But this Riley was—

"Meg? You getting in or what?" Riley stood beside the open passenger door, hands out, palms up, sunglasses firmly in place.

"Sorry," she mumbled and scrambled into the seat.

He slammed the door and marched around the hood, his face grim. She wanted to ask him about what had happened back there, but the shuttered look on his face told her he wasn't in a mood to share. How could she just let it drop? His breathing had grown heavy; he'd been sweating and rubbing his chest.

Without a word, he started the engine and pulled out of the gravel parking lot, the back tires kicking up stones as he pulled onto the main road.

Obviously, something bad had happened to him in Afghanistan, something to cause nightmares, something to cause his little episode at the church. Finding out what was wrong wasn't a matter of satisfying curiosity; she needed to think of Fiona. When Riley had left, they'd both still been so young, having an adult conversation or two now seemed reasonable.

She wished Riley would confide in her about his experiences in Afghanistan, so she could get to know and understand the man he was now.

He might get angry with her, but she had to try. "I know you don't want to talk, but I would like to understand what you're going through. You've gotten upset with me each time I've told people we were just neighbors or that you were a friend of Liam's, but how can I call you something more if you refuse to talk to me?"

He didn't say anything so she must've angered him. She twisted her hands together. Better to find out now that he didn't trust or care enough to—

Jerking the wheel sharply, he pulled into a parking spot in front of the hardware store. Heaving a deep sigh, he said, "It's not easy to talk about. I know I scared you with…with what happened today and that's the last thing I want to do. I thought talking with Travis before leaving would help and it did but not enough."

She reached across the middle console and touched his arm. He covered her hand with his.

"Some of the stuff I saw…over there…it changed me." He cleared his throat. "I think I have a handle on it, think I'm coping, and then something like today happens and I realize I'm Wile E. Coyote scrambling to gain traction in nothing but thin air."

She despised feeling so helpless, but anything she said would sound like meaningless platitudes. Maybe there was something she could do… It wasn't much but it was better than inaction. "Will you come for supper tonight?"

"What?"

She gave him an apologetic smile, understanding his surprise. "I'm inviting you to supper."

His gaze searched her face. "Supper?"

"Yes." Great, he thought she was making light of or ignoring what had happened. She needed to make him understand. "I've never been to war and I'm not a therapist but I can cook. I can feed you. When you offered me a glass of water during my asthma attack, you said it was because you had to do something." She sighed. "Well, that's how I feel."

His fingers tightened over hers. "Thanks. I'd love to come for supper."

Meg spent the afternoon catching up on laundry and checking on job openings in case the Loon Lake position didn't work out.

She squatted for a last minute check of her appearance in the stainless steel toaster on the counter before she answered the light knock at her door. As she hurried to let Riley in, she removed the hair tie and finger-combed her hair.

"Hey." Riley hovered in the doorway, his hair damp from the shower and his T-shirt stretched over his shoulders and biceps.

"Hey," she managed to reply, even though her saliva had dried up the minute she saw him. She rubbed her sweaty palms down the front of her pants. *Great. Dry mouth and wet hands—such a sexy combi— Stop right there. This is about offering friendship, nothing more.*

"I'm not too early, am I?" He shifted from one foot to the other.

"Oh, no, sorry. C'mon in." She stepped aside and led him into the kitchen.

His presence shrank the room, and as many times as he'd been in the cottage in the past, she shouldn't have been feeling awkward or shy, and yet she was.

She needed a distraction, so she grabbed the oven mitts off the counter and pulled the garlic bread from the oven, setting the aromatic slices on a plate.

He looked over her shoulder, inhaling deeply. "Mmm… can I help with anything?"

"No. It's…it's ready. Sit down while I dish it out." She fought the overwhelming urge to lean into him.

Riley pulled out a chair and sat at Meg's table, his gaze roaming around the cheerful kitchen. From the looks of it, Meg had spent considerable time and energy improving this room. The walls and old cabinets had a fresh coat of paint; the old porcelain sink gleamed under the rays of the sun shining through the window above it. He knew Meg's kitchen and the meal would be a memory he'd take back to Afghanistan. This sunny kitchen sure beat sitting in the dirt, his back resting against his full combat load and eating an MRE with a plastic spoon. Christ, what the hell was he thinking? His duty to his men should be his priority. It *was* his priority.

During supper they managed to keep the conversation going. He was mopping up the sauce from the chicken cacciatore on his plate with his garlic bread when Meg's cell phone chimed. She grabbed the phone from its charger on the counter.

After checking the screen, she said, "Sorry. I'm going to take this in the other room. I'll get some coffee to go with dessert in a minute."

She hadn't even looked up from her phone or waited for an answer before she left the room. He remembered a time when those green eyes had looked at him as if he were the most important person in her world.

His gut churned with the knowledge that he no longer had a place in her life. Supper had been what she said: the sharing of a meal. But that was the way it should be because he was going back to his men, his life, to the marines where he belonged. He didn't belong in Meg's kitchen eating home-cooked meals.

So why does it hurt to be excluded?

Riley jumped up and found dish liquid soap in the cabinet under the sink. Maybe washing the dishes would distract him from Meg's occasional laughter coming from the other room. He filled the sink and when the suds climbed halfway up the sides, he shut off the tap and plunged in.

"What're you doing?" Meg said as she came into the kitchen.

He half turned toward her. "Making myself useful."

"Washing dishes?"

"Why not?" He made a show of looking around. "Did I miss a dishwasher here somewhere?"

"No." She picked up a towel, pulled a dish out of the rinse water and began drying a dinner plate with quick, economical movements. "It's on my list of improvements."

Her small, capable hands caught his attention. Meg didn't wear rings or even have polish on her nails, but her hands were infinitely feminine. A shaft of lust jolted through him and coiled low in his belly. He ached to feel those hands on him, touching him, exploring him. *What're you, Cooper? Sixteen?* He pressed against the sink, hoping to hide the evidence of his arousal.

Get a grip on this, Marine. No distractions. This time was for healing, not hooking up with Meggie again. She deserved more than what he could give her. As a distraction, he studied the cabinets surrounding the sink, wondering about the potential placement of a dishwasher. Plumbing was a much safer topic than Meg's hands and what they could do to him.

He grabbed a scrubber from the ceramic frog on the

windowsill above the sink. "It looks to me like you're doing a good job with the place."

"Thanks." Her face creased into a proud smile, making her green eyes sparkle.

"Do you have a list of what else needs attention?" *What're you doing? Do not get involved.*

"You've already done too much."

"I'll take a look around." He had noticed a loose step on the porch and a shutter that needed to be reattached. The roof looked as though it could use some attention, too.

"That's not necessary. It might take a while, but I'm capable and I'm not in a rush." She pulled out the drawer, rattling the silverware inside. "I plan on being here a good, long while."

"I'm not doubting your capabilities. I simply want to help." What happened to not getting involved? He knew what was expected of him as a marine. The routine and belonging gave him the security he'd lacked as a child. So why did an image of being in this kitchen with Meg and her daughter keep popping into his head? Considering the battleground his parents had created, he had no business thinking he could be a family man. He shoved those thoughts aside.

"Thanks. I'll think about it." She pushed the drawer in with her hip. "How about taking our coffee and dessert onto the porch? The mosquitoes haven't been too bad yet. We may as well enjoy it."

"Sounds good." He dried his hands on the towel she handed him.

"I'm calling it dessert but it's just some homemade cookies," she said and pulled out a decorative tin and opened it. "I hope you like snickerdoodles. They're Fiona's favorite."

"I haven't had any in ages, but the ones my gran made were always my favorite as a kid. Fiona has good taste." He had fond memories of visits to his maternal grandmother. She never harangued him over his father's supposed infidelities or his mother's spending habits. Gran insisted he be allowed to be a child and not a confidant for either parent's shortcomings.

"Yes…well…" Meg ducked her head and pulled out a box of coffee pods.

Even though she'd already put cookies on a plate to bring out, he snagged a handful from the open tin and winked when she raised her eyebrows. Snickerdoodles were comfort food as far as he was concerned and he'd never get enough. And cookies weren't the only thing in this kitchen he couldn't get enough of. That thought weighed heavy on him as he followed Meg onto the porch.

They settled in the Adirondack chairs and sipped their coffee in silence for a few minutes.

She set her mug on the little table separating the chairs. "What made you come to Loon Lake?"

"I had thirty days and wanted someplace where I could relax and…" His voice trailed off. He didn't know himself why he'd picked it other than to relive some good memories.

"And drink the bottles in your bag?"

He grimaced. "To be honest, I'm not sure why I brought them. I haven't opened any."

"You're over twenty-one and don't owe me any explanations." She sipped her coffee.

"Why did *you* pick Loon Lake over staying closer to Boston?"

"Because it's where I want to raise Fiona and it's a

good home for us." Her gaze wandered over the yard, her beautiful green eyes bright, a proud expression on her face. "I have plans."

"Plans?" He grabbed the last snickerdoodle, glanced at her and snapped the cookie, offering her half.

Munching on the cookie, she surveyed the yard as if she was a Realtor. "I can picture a swing set for Fiona... maybe a dog. That would have been harder in the city. Liam bought a triple-decker in Dorchester and wanted me to move into the second- or third-floor apartment, but his backyard is the size of a postage stamp...half of it concrete. He's on a nice street, but I wouldn't have felt comfortable letting Fiona out to run around with a puppy."

"A dog? What about your asthma?" Aw, Christ, the sudden sadness in her eyes punched him in the gut. Why did he bring that up? "I shouldn't have said that."

She squeezed her hand into a fist. "The doctor said if I could find something hypoallergenic, it would be okay. I hate to deny Fiona because of my asthma."

"I'm sorry. Do you think you'll be able to find one?"

"They exist. I just have to find the right one for both of us."

He reached out and took her clenched hand in both of his and uncurled her fingers one by one. Tracing the lines, he stroked her palm with his index finger. "I guess I'm still wrapping my head around the fact that you're all grown up and a mother. Does it feel weird living in your parents' old place? I left a wet towel on the floor and I swear I heard my mother yelling at me to pick it up."

"Yeah, at first it felt really weird. Especially when I started making changes." She gave him a lopsided grin that sent his blood racing. "Like you, I heard my mom's voice in my head asking why I chose *that* color for the kitchen."

He curled his fingers over hers and they shared a laugh.

"Riley, I—"

Meg's words were cut off by a shrill *a-hink-a-honk-a-hink-a-honk*. Moments later, geese flying in the standard V formation filled the clear sky above them. They watched the giant birds until the large flock had disappeared.

"Let's walk down to the lake." He tugged on her hand. "I know how you used to love to listen to the loons at sunset."

She hesitated.

He pulled on her hand again. "C'mon, for old times' sake. Whaddaya say?"

"I… Yes, let me grab my jacket."

"I'll bring in the coffee cups while you do that." Her agreement to walk to the lake with him shouldn't have meant as much as it did. It was nothing and yet he looked forward to it like a teenager looked forward to some backseat time with the prettiest girl in the school.

Coward.

The word flashed in her mind as she walked toward the lake. She'd started to confess when the geese flew over. She shouldn't have let that stop her. Nor should she have postponed it when he suggested a walk to the lake. No doubt about it. She was a coward.

Dusk had settled around them by the time they reached the lake. The sun had dipped below the horizon, but there was still enough light for Meg to see the conical spires of the trees silhouetted against the sky. Most of the lake was obscured, shrouded in fog rising from the water. Her heart beat faster the closer they got. Being afraid of something after dark that she was comfortable with during the light of day was silly, maybe childish, but telling herself that didn't help or make it go away. But then, that was the definition of an *irrational fear*.

Riley's hand landed on her shoulder, startling her, and her toes curled in her sneakers.

He bent down so his mouth was close to her ear, his warm, moist breath tickling her. "Take a nice, deep breath and let it out…slowly. You're safe. I promise."

"I'm okay." She sucked in another breath and jammed her hands into the front pocket of the new hoodie Riley had bought for her at the hospital.

"I'd forgotten your fear of getting too close to the water at night. But you know you have nothing to worry about. You're not going to fall in and even if you did, this time you know how to swim."

The concern in his deep voice caused her heart to expand. "It's okay… I've… I've outgrown it."

"That's good to know, but just like when we were kids, I'll jump in after you if you fall." His arms went around her and he pulled her closer, her back to his chest. She leaned against him, unable to help herself. She wanted to blame the way she melted into him all on her fear of the dark water, but she knew it wasn't totally true. His heat and hardness drew her to him. They stood locked in an embrace, his chin resting on her head.

The first time she'd broken out of her stereotypical role as the family's good child who followed the rules was the day after the family had arrived at their new vacation home. She and Tina had taken a borrowed rowboat onto the lake after dark. Meg had fallen into the dark water and panicked. If not for Riley, she might have drowned. He'd seen her sneaking out and followed her, so he'd been there to save her. The next time she'd thrown off her good-girl mantle had been the night she'd spent in Riley's arms. But he hadn't been there later to help her. So she'd learned to save herself. Not that she hadn't nearly drowned—figuratively, that is—a few times, but she'd managed to tread water and build a good life here.

A long, mournful wail echoed eerily over the water. Seconds later there was another distinctive tremolo call, as if to answer the first one. Water splashed and the evocative calls continued to punctuate the night air.

"They're calling to their mates," he whispered roughly before turning her in his arms. His lips captured hers and a spark of desire shot through her entire body, right down to her soul. She heard a low moan and wasn't sure if the sound came from her, him or the loons. With his lips over hers, she tasted coffee and cinnamon from the cookies.

She arched her back, trying to get closer, trying to mold her lips to his, her desire to his. His arms tightened around her in response, as if he wanted to melt into her, or absorb her into himself. She fisted her hands in his soft T-shirt, leaning into him when her legs could no longer support her weight. *Remember what happened last time*, a little voice inside warned. True, but she deserved some excitement and, just like she knew how to swim now, she also knew enough to stop before things got out of control.

He made a low, rumbling sound deep in his throat and she pressed closer as heat and moisture rushed to the juncture at her thighs. *Yeah, what was that about know-*

ing when to put the brakes on? She needed to remember he wasn't staying in Loon Lake. Had she learned nothing? She was not one of those loons and Riley was not her *mate* for life, not even for now. He'd be gone within thirty days.

She drew her head back and pushed on his chest. "Riley, I can't."

"Is there someone else?"

"No. No one." Shaking her head, she took another step back.

"Is it the guy who—"

She crossed her arms over her chest. "This has nothing to do with anyone else but me. I have responsibilities. I can't afford to do temporary."

"That's all I can do."

"I know." She exhaled slowly.

"Meggie, I—"

"I get it. The marines are your life." She'd tried, and failed, to keep a note of wistfulness out of her voice. She turned and trudged back toward the cottages as the loons continued to call to their mates.

Chapter Five

Meg stuck the red-handled trowel into the loose dirt and wiggled it around before pushing the small clump of purple pansies into the hole. It was probably too early even for pansies, but she'd needed a distraction while she rehearsed how to tell Riley he was a father. She should've told him last night when they'd walked to the lake. He might not be staying in Loon Lake, but while he was here it was only fair for father and daughter to get acquainted. Compared to telling Riley, breaking the news to her parents had been a cinch.

"Need some help?"

The garden tool slipped from her hand and she turned to face Riley. "Perfect timing. I was just finishing up."

"I figured if I waited long enough, you'd be done." He grinned and held out his hand to help her up from her kneeling position. "Seriously, is there something I can do?"

She wiped her hands on her frayed jeans. "You could fill the watering can over there from the exterior faucet on the side of the house."

"I guess I can handle that." He picked up the can and went to the spigot. "Got any of those cookies left?"

She rolled her eyes, hoping lightening the mood would also settle those elephants—she'd gone way past butterflies—tramping around in her stomach since kissing him last night. "I guess. You water the flowers while I go wash my hands and get the cookies. I suppose you'll want some coffee with them."

"You read my mind."

She put a K-cup into the coffeemaker and went to wash her face and run a comb through her hair. While the second cup was brewing, she put some of the cookies on a plate.

"Give those mugs to me and I'll take them out on the porch," he said from the doorway.

"Oh, sure, you're Johnny-on-the-spot when food is involved."

He wiggled his eyebrows. "I'm not an idiot."

Once seated in the Adirondack chairs, Meg sipped her coffee and searched for the courage to tell Riley the truth.

He leaned back in the chair and brought a leg up, resting his ankle on the opposite knee.

She drew in a breath. Okay, she should tell him now, while they were alone and both relaxed. "Riley, there's something I—"

Bugles blaring the opening strains of the Marine Corps Hymn interrupted her. He held up a finger as he dug his cell phone out of his pocket and frowned. "Damn. I should get this."

She nodded and sat back in the chair. A reprieve, that was all this was.

He stood. "What's up?"

He didn't say anything else, but the color drained from his face as he listened. When he caught her watching him, he turned on his heel and strode to the other end of the porch, keeping his back to her.

She nibbled on her bottom lip. Obviously, it wasn't good news, although his end of the conversation consisted of a few "uh-huhs" and a lot of head shaking. By the time he ended the call, she could bounce pennies off his rigid back.

"Riley?" She rose and went to him, touching his shoulder, but he shrugged off her hand. "Is something wrong?"

"Some bad news about one of the guys in my squad," he said without turning around.

"Do you… Would you like to talk about it?"

"A guy I served with ate his gun today." He turned and marched back to the chair but didn't sit; instead, he slammed his phone down on the table. The coffee mugs and cookie plate rattled. "I don't think talking is going to change anything."

"No, but sometimes it helps," she said in an even tone, refusing to take his anger personally. She put her hands in her pockets to keep from reaching out. What else did she have to offer besides comfort? Would he even accept it?

"Tell that to his wife and two little girls." He held up both hands. "I'm sorry, Meggie, I… We'll talk later, okay?"

Her heart stuttered at the pain he must be feeling. Her

shoulders slumping, she turned back to the table and noticed he'd left his phone. "Riley, wait."

He waved his hand. "Not now, Meg."

"No, you left your phone." She ran to catch up to him, but hesitated when he turned around. Seeing him suffering made her want to throw her arms around him and help ease his pain. But she held back.

"I'm sorry." He stepped closer and wrapped his large hand over hers, tugging her close. His intense gaze met hers as he leaned over and gave her a quick, hard kiss. "I'm not going to be good company right now."

For a long time after he'd left, she sat on the porch, her knees drawn up to her chest. What if that had been Riley? The thought of something happening to him before he even had a chance to meet Fiona gutted her. Unshed tears scalded the back of her throat. Father and daughter had a right to know one another and she'd never forgive herself if she could have brought that about and didn't.

After a sleepless night, Meg poured a second cup of coffee. She'd resisted staring out the window at Riley's cottage, and had succeeded...a few of those times.

She yawned and stared at the coffee in her cup as if it could provide an answer to her problems. Telling Riley the truth was job number one. Yeah, as soon as she figured out how.

A knock at her door interrupted her thoughts and she jumped up to answer.

"Hey." Riley stood on her porch with a tentative smile and a bag from a coffee shop on the square. He lifted the bag. "I hope you still like the cheese Danish from Millie's Bakery."

"I do."

"Is that coffee I smell?" He lifted an eyebrow.

She stepped aside. "C'mon in."

In the kitchen, Riley set the bag on the table. "Sit. I can fix my own coffee."

Meg opened the bag and peered at the three assorted Danish. "How come you didn't get any for yourself?"

He turned around, mug in hand and his mouth slightly open. She laughed and plopped in her seat. "Gotcha."

He sat down across from her. "Lucky for you, I'm willing to share."

"Me? You're the one who's lucky because I'm so generous." She pulled out a Danish, put it on a napkin and pushed it toward him before getting one for herself. If only she didn't have the guilt hanging over her head, she might be able to enjoy her favorite pastry.

"I came over this morning to try to explain," he said before taking a bite.

She nodded, but remained silent while he chewed, afraid of saying the wrong thing. It was hard to even imagine what he might be going through, especially after what he'd told her after his episode at the church. She'd understood on a certain level. There were times when she'd felt as though she were scrambling for traction in thin air when it came to being a single parent and wanting to do her best, but being on a battlefield was beyond her experiences.

He scrubbed a hand over his face. "I've lost guys on the battlefield and that stinks, but losing them this way—" he shook his head "—is worse. Ya know? It feels…senseless. I mourn them, but I can't let myself wallow or that's all I'd do. The best way to honor their memory is to move on and find a way to help those still here. Help them find ways to cope with severe PTSD. I hate it that some see suicide as the only way out. Does that make sense? Or make me seem heartless?"

"Oh, Riley," Meg whispered and laid her hand over the one he had resting on the table. "I saw what you did for Travis at the church."

"You mean the guy in the boonie hat?" He frowned. "I didn't do anything except talk and I'm not sure what good that did."

"I saw him smile and relax while you were talking to him. And he hung around for a while. Usually he's got one foot out the door."

He shrugged as if it was nothing. "We just talked."

"Yeah, but sometimes little things can make a big difference." He might downplay what he did, but she saw that he had connected with Travis, something none of the others had been able to do.

"Now you sound like Ogle."

"Oh, dear Lord." Meg burst out laughing and he joined her. Times like this she spotted the old Riley under the layers the years had piled on. But she had to admit, this Riley was terrific, too. *And temporary. Don't forget temporary.*

He finished his pastry and wiped the crumbs off his hands. "Would you go out with me?"

She choked on the sip of coffee she'd taken. Did she hear that right? Was he asking her out?

He leaned closer. "You okay?"

She nodded vigorously and cleared her throat. "What do you mean by *out*?"

"What most people mean. A date."

"A date?" Could she do it? Go on a date and not fall in love all over again?

He glanced around. "Is there an echo in here?"

"Sorry. I wanted to be sure we were on the same page." What harm could one date do? She glanced at the picture of her and Fiona on the front of her refrigerator.

"Is that a yes?"

She was an adult now, not a hormone-pumped teenager. Surely she could handle a date. "Yeah...sure."

"How about Angelo's for dinner and dancing?"

Yeah, he was serious. "Angelo's?"

"There's that echo again."

The Italian restaurant was a favorite of couples... not that she'd had dates since she'd been in Loon Lake. Maybe it was time to be a bit selfish. "Sorry. But I'm not sure what brought this on."

"Well, I wasn't pleasant yesterday and since it's my fault you're a subject of gossip, I thought—"

"So this is a pity date?" She swallowed hard.

"What? No." He blew out his breath. "Can't a guy want to take a beautiful girl on a date?"

Riley yanked on the tie and pulled out the knot, only to start over. What had possessed him to ask Meg on a formal date? He'd had to run out that afternoon to buy dress pants, a button-down shirt, a tie and even shoes. He wasn't a suit guy. At funerals or weddings of his fellow marines, he'd worn his dress blues. Lately, there'd been far too many of the former, like the one he'd have to attend soon. Was there something he could've done? That question had haunted him ever since the phone call.

When and where had he lost the ability to tie a necktie? Impatient with himself, he pushed the maudlin thoughts aside and began the steps for a Windsor knot all over again. Tonight belonged to Meg. He would concentrate on their date—something they'd never done. The night they'd hooked up, Meg had offered to give him a lift.

Thinking about his own mortality had him wondering if Meggie would remember him as the guy who'd made her the butt of local gossip. Dinner and dancing at Angelo's wasn't leaving a legacy, but he wanted to give her a good memory and show the rest of Loon Lake that he respected Meg. And preferably that he'd accomplish all this without a clip-on tie.

Finally satisfied with his knot, he grabbed his wallet off the dresser and stuffed it into his back pocket. Crazy thing was, despite the hassle of having to dress the part, he was looking forward to spending an evening with Meg. He might not be right for her, but for tonight he could pretend. For once in his life, he could be "that guy" for Meggie.

He'd barely knocked at her door when she flung it open and he swallowed his tongue. A short black dress and sexy heels showed off her long, shapely legs, and she'd piled her hair into a mass of copper curls on top of her head. She smiled shyly at him while he waited for his stupid heart to start pumping again.

Her smile slipped. "Is everything okay?"

"Your lips are all shiny." *Wow, such a smooth talker there, Marine.*

"Is that a problem?"

"No, you look beautiful. Stunning." *Too good for the likes of you.*

She grinned, her eyes gleaming with humor, warming him. "You clean up pretty well, too."

"They're new…my clothes, that is." *Oh, God, I need to shut up.*

She laughed. "So are mine."

"Meg, you better not tell me you walked into town." He made a mental note to talk to Ogle Whatley about getting Meg another car before he left. *Yeah, that's right. Don't forget you're leaving.* He shoved that thought to the back of his mind. Tonight belonged to Meg. And so did he.

"No, my friend Tina took me shopping and dressed me." She blushed. "I mean, she helped me pick out the dress."

At least he wasn't the only one tripping over their tongue tonight, which made him determined to do this right for Meggie. He held out his arm. "Shall we?"

Riley tried to concentrate on his driving and not the beautiful, sexy woman beside him. Yup, no doubt about it: Meg was all grown up. The whole time in Afghanistan, when he'd allowed himself to think about Meg, she'd been nineteen. Now she was a woman. A very desirable woman who deserved the white picket fence and a man who would be there for her, day in and day out, not half a world away. He couldn't give her a lot of things, but he could give her tonight.

He slowed the pickup as they approached the restaurant's parking lot...the almost deserted parking lot. *What the...?*

"You didn't book the whole place, did you?"

"No." He braked near the entrance. "I made a reservation, that's all."

"So, they're open or supposed to be."

"Supposed to be," he echoed and put the truck into Park. "Wait here. Let me check it out."

He jumped out of the truck, a sick feeling forming in the pit of his stomach as he approached the building.

* * *

Meg smoothed her dress over her thighs and smiled. No matter what happened tonight, she'd achieved her dream of a LBD and killer heels. Sure, she had trouble walking in the heels, let alone dancing, but the look of male appreciation on Riley's face made the pinched toes worthwhile. Tonight she felt like a princess from one of Fiona's videos. Tomorrow she'd come clean to Riley, but tonight would be hers, a memory to tuck away and pull out when life got rough. Tonight she was Cinderella.

He trudged back to the truck and got in. Sighing, he rubbed his face. "They had a kitchen fire this afternoon and will be closed while they clean up. Meggie, I'm so sorry. We'll look for someplace else."

"It's okay. I don't mind where we go."

After trying two other places that were booked and turning people away, he banged his palm against the steering wheel. "I had this big night planned for you. Now we don't even have somewhere to eat."

She reached over and squeezed the bunched muscles on his forearm. "It's not your fault. I have an idea. Why don't we stop at a drive-through and get some burgers and fries and drive to the beach at the lake? They've got picnic tables. We can eat under the stars."

"I wanted to give you a real date, a good memory."

"Who says that's not a real date?"

"But you're all dressed up."

"I dressed like this for you and you're right here." She slipped her hand over his and he turned his over to twine his fingers with hers. Tonight was her night, probably the only one she was going to get, and she was determined to enjoy it, no matter what. Tomorrow there would be plenty of time for confessions. "So how about it?"

On the way to the beach, Riley stopped at the Pic-N-Save but wouldn't let her come in with him. He came back out with several bags but stowed them on the back-seat.

"This isn't the way I planned this," he muttered as he took the bag from the kid working the drive-through window and handed it to her.

"I know but I'm flexible." Motherhood had taught—no, tonight was all about her and storing up memories for when Riley left. She'd honor her obligation as Fiona's mom tomorrow.

The tires crunched on the crushed gravel parking lot at the lake. Riley chose a spot and turned to her. "You wait here a minute."

"Sit? Stay?" She raised her eyebrows in mock anger, but her lips twitched with the effort to suppress a smile.

"You're not gonna let me live that down, are you?"

She laughed, shaking her head. "Not a chance."

Chuckling, he grabbed the bags from the back and jogged toward the picnic area. She tried to see what he was doing, but where he'd parked made that difficult. Opening the bag with their supper, she plopped a curly fry in her mouth. The truck smelled like their food but underneath was the scent of Riley's spicy aftershave. As a teenager, she'd swiped one of Riley's shirts when he'd gone swimming with Liam. She'd kept the shirt hidden in her drawer and would take it out and bury her nose in Riley's aroma.

He came back and opened her door. "Let me help you down."

She set the food on the floor and held out a hand, but he ignored her hand and seized her around the waist. He clutched her against his warmth before easing her to the ground. Then he grabbed the bag with their food and took her hand.

Her heart swelled. The picnic table was set with a tablecloth, candles and a mason jar with a bouquet of fresh flowers.

"It's not Angelo's but…" He shrugged and cleared his throat.

"It's better." She squeezed his hand. "It's just the two of us."

After she'd settled on the bench seat, he sat next to her, his thigh brushing against hers. Sitting next to him like this, it was hard to remember all the reasons Riley wasn't the man for her.

They ate their burgers and reminisced about summers spent at the lake.

They were almost finished when he reached over and wiped his napkin on her cheek. "Mustard."

"Thanks," she whispered, her gaze clashing with his.

Riley cleared his throat and began gathering their trash. "I'll throw this stuff away."

"Let me help."

"No. You sit there. This evening wasn't supposed to involve you having to clean up."

She bumped her shoulder against his. "It's not your fault. And you made it special with the flowers and candles."

"It's the least I could do," he said as he threw their trash in the covered barrel. "Wait right there," Riley called to her as he went to his truck. Music drifted back to her.

He came back to the picnic table and reached out his hand. "I believe I promised dancing."

She took his hand but remained seated. "I'm not sure

I can manage in these shoes. How about just sitting here listening to the music and watching the sun set and the stars come out?"

"Thank God." He squeezed her hand and grinned, deepening his sexy-beyond-belief dimples. "Because I can't dance."

"We can sit at the end of the dock if you'd like. We can still hear the music," she said.

He glanced over at the wooden dock that reached out into the lake. "Will you be okay that close to the water? It's getting dark."

"As long as you're beside me, I'll be okay. But first, let me take these shoes off. At least now I know why they're called killer heels."

After she'd slipped off the shoes, he took her hand again and they strolled over to the dock. When they reached the end, he sat down beside her and dangled his legs next to hers.

"You okay?" he asked as the sun dipped below the horizon and disappeared with a wink.

"I'm okay," she said, but her voice wasn't as strong as she'd wanted.

Wrapping his arm around her, he pulled her closer. Their gazes met and locked and she knew this was the romantic moment she'd spent her teen years dreaming about. These tender moments weren't lustful or frenzied like the night they'd created Fiona; this was sweet and slow, almost reverent.

His lips touching hers was achingly gentle, the culmination of all her girlish fantasies. This was Rick and Ilsa, Westley and Buttercup. The years of cynicism melted away and she believed in fairy tales again.

His firm lips eased away from hers, but he rubbed his

nose against hers and brought his hand up to caress the back of her neck. They drew apart to watch the stars, but he kept his arm around her, anchoring her against his warmth.

He squeezed her shoulder and pointed to a trail of light blazing across the sky. "Falling star. Make a wish."

"I already did." She leaned into his solid warmth, enjoying their time together. The evening hadn't gone as planned, but this was more intimate.

"Wishing we'd gone to Angelo's?"

"Nope. I think tonight was perfect." And she meant it.

He raised an eyebrow. "Even if no one got to see you in your dress and those sexy shoes?"

"You're the only one that mattered," she whispered.

Rustling noises followed by chattering interrupted their moment.

Riley glanced back toward the picnic tables. "Raccoons. Maybe that's our cue to leave."

"Yeah, I think the kitchen fire was enough of an interesting footnote for tonight."

He stood and held out his hand to help her up. She nestled her hand in his, knowing tonight would be a memory she'd cherish forever, no matter what happened between them in the future.

The next morning, the first thing Meg did was look across the yard. His truck was gone. She told herself he probably had some errands in town. No big deal. Surely after last night he wouldn't leave without telling her. But by midafternoon when he still hadn't come back, she had to face the truth. She'd allowed herself to weave dreams and hopes out of thin air. He'd made no promises, including the chaste kiss when he dropped her at her door at the end of the evening.

Face it, Meg, that kiss—heck, the whole darn evening—meant more to you than to him.

Did she think a sexy dress and shoes could change him into a home-every-night-for-supper family man? *The marines are my life now, Meggie.*

Calling herself all kinds of a fool, she pulled out her phone.

Thank you for last night.

She could imagine her mother chastising her. *No, Ma, I'm not chasing him. I'm being polite.*

Her phone dinged back.

Sorry didn't go as planned.

She nibbled her lower lip trying to decide how to answer.

I enjoyed it.

No answering ding. Being concerned wasn't the same as stalking.

Where are you?

Funeral.

She squeezed her phone. The fellow marine who'd committed suicide.

She typed, I'm so sorry wish I could help...

For the next three days Mother Nature matched her mood with gray skies and intermittent rain. Thanks to Riley she didn't have to worry about her basement. Not only had he and Kevin put a waterproof coating on, but they'd also installed a sump pump for good measure. Unfortunately, neither one of those improvements helped her leaky roof.

She could only assume Riley was spending time with his fellow marines after losing one of their own. And while she couldn't fault him for that, the more time that passed, the harder it would be to tell him about Fiona and the guiltier she felt.

"If it wasn't for bad luck, you'd have no luck at all," she muttered as she emptied the saucepan she'd put down in the middle of the night to catch the drips from her leaky roof. Last time she'd been in the shed, she'd noticed a blue tarp. Time to go and see if it was still there, and if so, was it still serviceable.

Getting the tarp and an aluminum ladder from the shed, she set about fixing the problem. She knew if she called her friend Brody Wilson, he would come and help, but this was her house, her problem, her solution.

"What in God's name do you think you're doing?"

Chapter Six

Startled by Riley's angry voice, Meg lost her grip on the tarp she'd dragged to the roof. She scrambled to catch it, but her fingers couldn't hold on to the slippery blue plastic. She watched helplessly as the weather-resistant cover slid down the pitch of her roof, no doubt further damaging the worn shingles on its way. When had he gotten back? She looked over at the cottage and sure enough, his black F-150 sat out front.

Last night, listening to the steady drip of water into the stainless steel pan, she'd hatched what seemed like a good plan. But last night's brilliance was turning into Meg's Folly in the light of day. And of course Riley had to return in time to witness it. Yep, bad luck all the way.

"Stay right there. Don't move," Riley ordered and adjusted the aluminum ladder against the roof with a clatter.

She ignored him and inched her way forward. "You need to get a dog. I think that sit and stay stuff works better with canines."

"Sweet Jesus, woman, you're giving me heart failure." His voice got closer as he made his way up the ladder, muttering colorful and unique curses. "What are you doing up here?"

"Admiring the view." She ordered her heart to quit thumping so hard every time he acted as if he cared about her. Her errant tarp appeared over the edge of the roof, followed by a large male hand plunking it down and holding it in place.

Riley hauled himself over the side and onto the roof. "Can I offer some useful advice?"

"Can you spare it?"

"I'm not in the mood, Meg."

She glared at him. "Neither am I."

"Other than breaking your neck, what did you hope to accomplish up here?"

"I was trying to use the tarp as a temporary solution. The roof is leaking." She reached for the bright blue plastic. "Thanks. I can take it from here."

He held the tarp out of reach. "I'll take care of it. You go down before you kill yourself."

"This Neanderthal act of yours is getting old." She'd love nothing more than to let him take care of things, but she couldn't count on it. If you didn't expect things, you couldn't be disappointed. She'd had enough disappointment when it came to Riley. She'd done her best to be understanding about his disappearance after his friend's funeral, but he hadn't once tried to contact her. Would a short text just to let her know he was okay have killed him? She groaned at her own poor choice of words. If she wasn't careful she'd have herself convinced he cared about her, and she'd be weaving fairy-tale endings that weren't going to happen. The only fairy tales she allowed in her life were the ones she read to Fiona.

"That's too bad but I'm up here now, and I'm putting an end to your nonsense." He unfolded the tarp. "Where is it leaking?"

She wasn't letting him get away with talking to her like that. Forgiveness wasn't on her agenda at the moment. Putting her hands on her hips, she demanded. "Since when is preventing water damage nonsense?"

"The sane response would be to call a roofer." He shook the tarp.

"Oh? Well, then, it's a good thing you're here to save me from myself."

"Christ, Meghan, I'm serious."

"So am I. I've managed to survive twenty-five years without your help, so you can go home or disappear for another three days."

"Is that what this is about?"

Was it? "No. This is about my leaky roof and nothing more."

"These are pretty brittle." He squatted down and flipped a few shingles. The loosened granules rolled down the slope, sounding like sand pouring out of a bucket.

What was wrong with her? He was examining asphalt shingles and she was imagining that hand holding hers while they sat at the end of the dock and counted the stars. She needed to stop this, and her hormones needed to go back into the hibernation they'd been in before Riley arrived.

"Is it?" He glanced at her.

Oh, God. She'd been so busy fantasizing, she hadn't been paying attention to what he'd asked. "Is what… what?"

He rubbed his hand across his mouth. "This is not the place for that."

Her heart pounded and she rubbed her palms on her jeans. Trying for casual, she asked, "For what?"

"You have to ask?" He cocked his eyebrow. "Okay, I'll play. For the way you're looking at me."

She shook her head and reached again for the tarp. "I don't know what you mean."

"Yeah, you keep telling yourself that."

Heat spread across her face and she yanked on the blue plastic. Maybe, if she told herself enough times, she'd believe it herself. "Are you going to help me get this tarp on?"

"The sooner, the better." He sighed. "I don't like you up here."

What about on the porch? Or at the lake?

She pushed those thoughts aside as he helped her spread the tarp, tucking it under the shingles at the top. If he wasn't going to mention their date, then neither was she. When he reached his hand out, she handed him the roofing nails from her pocket along with the hammer she'd hooked into the waistband of her jeans.

After he secured the tarp, he said, "I'll check around for any other trouble spots. You go down. Now."

"There are parts over the porch that are—"

"I'm sorry, Meghan, did I give you the impression I was asking when I said, 'Go down'?"

"I'm not one of your marines you can order around."

"Yeah, they follow my orders." Riley gripped the top of the ladder and lifted his chin.

Of all the...

She sputtered as she made her way down the ladder, but she wasn't angry. Although she'd never admit it out loud, she found his protectiveness sexy. Despite what she'd told him that night at the lake when she'd called a halt to their kiss, she was tempted to do temporary.

Bold talk for someone who'd let opportunity slip through her hands, she thought regretfully.

Riley held his breath as she climbed down the ladder, not sucking in air until she'd reached the bottom.

He surveyed the roof, wondering if he had enough time to replace it before he left. The thought of her up here trying to patch a leak while he was half a world away made his stomach roll.

Unfortunately, trying to haul stacks of shingles up here could wrench his shoulder and if that happened, he might never get back to his men. And he didn't want anything to get in the way of reuniting with his squad.

Not even the lovely Meg?

He told his inner voice to shut up. Of course he wanted to get back to his men as soon as possible. Even though Meg had been in his thoughts those three days, spending time with his fellow marines at the funeral had strengthened his commitment. Hadn't it? He wouldn't dishonor himself, his men, or his commitment. And what about the men who died? He needed to honor them if nothing else. *But you've already given the corps years. Isn't that enough?*

Riley growled and stomped over to the part of the roof that hung over the porch. *Crack.* A rotted board gave under his weight. Shards of wood scraped his legs as he passed between the joists. Now that was a dumbass move. No wonder he was waist deep in Meg's roof.

"Riley? Are you okay?"

"Found one of those weak spots in the roof." He braced his hands on the shingles, the mineral granules digging into his palms, and moved his foot around until he found a rafter. He gave a push with his feet and hands, intending to boost himself back up. Instead the decayed materials snapped. Oh, Christ, he was going down.

What was underneath? He gritted his teeth against the inevitable fall, after which he landed square on one of the Adirondack chairs, which groaned under the impact and then gave up the fight.

Flat on his back on a pile of rotted boards, he spat and wiped dust and splinters off his face. The wood and dust smelled like mushrooms. Dry rot. He let off a string of curses in his head. The adrenaline pumping through him was helping stave off the pain, but he knew from experience he would soon be in a world of hurt.

"Oh! My! God!"

The panic in her voice brought his head up, which sent a shard of pain through his ribs.

"Riley? Oh, my God, you're bleeding." She dropped to her knees beside him, running her hands over his ripped shirt, inspecting the cuts on his arms and chest. Oh, man, this wasn't a good time for that particular piece of anatomy to be coming to life. Gotta love all that excess adrenaline. When she skimmed over his shoulder, he bit back a curse.

Grunting, he drew in a breath, and a groan slipped out before he could stop it. "I'm okay. Got the wind knocked out of me."

Her hands continued their journey, searching for injuries. "Don't move. Something could be broken."

"Only my pride," he muttered. He scrubbed his hand over his face and then through his hair, sending a shower of dust and dirt into the air. He coughed, cursing under his breath when excruciating pain stabbed him in the ribs.

"Meggie, I'm…" He ground his teeth against the pain. *Don't wimp out now, Marine. Keep it together—you're scaring her.*

He moved his legs, breathing out a sigh of relief when they obeyed without difficulty. "I might need some assistance to stand up."

Meg leaned forward. "I don't want to hurt you."

"You won't."

He rubbed his hand over the right side of his chest. Pressed. Ground his teeth. "I think I may have bruised a few ribs."

Eyes round, she pulled her phone from the back pocket of her jeans. "You could have a punctured lung, internal injuries." She swiped her thumb over the screen.

He frowned. "What are you doing?"

"Calling 911. You need an ambulance."

He grabbed the phone out of her hand. "You're overreacting. I didn't fall that far."

She gaped at him, glanced pointedly at the huge hole in the porch roof and then the shattered pile of wood that had once been a chair. "It's not the fall I'm concerned about—it's the landing."

She held her hand out for the phone but he shoved it in the front pocket of his jeans, earning an exasperated sigh from her.

"I don't care what you say, Riley Cooper. I'm taking you to the hospital."

"No."

Still on her knees beside him, she spoke through her teeth. "I'm serious. You could have a ruptured spleen or internal bleeding." She held out her hand again. "Give. Me. The. Phone."

"No internal bleeding, I promise." *I hope.* He braced his hands in another attempt to rise but his shoulder protested and his left hand failed to support his weight. Frowning, he lifted it and gave his wrist an experimental twist, but pain made the movement limited, and it was beginning to swell. Huh, that couldn't be good. "But I might need to have this looked at."

"Your poor wrist." Her hand flew to her mouth. "It could be broken. That's it. I'm calling an ambulance. Give me the phone."

"Hey, it takes more than a fall from a roof to stop me."

She closed her eyes and made a choking sound.

He touched her face. "Hey, hey, I will go to have the wrist looked at, but I refuse to go by ambulance. We can take my truck."

Opening her eyes, she stared at him, her eye freckles dark against the green-gold. "You shouldn't be driving."

It was on the tip of his tongue to protest, but she was right. "You can drive."

"Your truck?" She shook her head. "I'm not sure that's such a good idea."

"I trust you."

She started to rise. "I'll get my purse. I... I'm sorry I ever started this."

"Hey." He grabbed her hand with his good one. "It's

not your fault. I knew better than to step without checking first."

He didn't tell her anger had made him careless. How could he even contemplate not returning to his men? How could he protect them from here? How could he protect Meg from Afghanistan? Since when did he consider protecting Meg his job? The fall must have rattled a few screws loose.

She bit her bottom lip and he wanted to lick the spot her teeth had touched. *Really, Cooper, you're going there now?*

She glanced at his hand clasping hers.

He gripped her hand as if his life depended on it. Yep, definitely knocked some screws loose. He let go and she scrambled away. "I'll get my purse."

At the door, she glanced back. "Sit. Stay."

His laugh turned into a groan. "Do I get a treat if I do?"

"Maybe that could be arranged," she tossed at him before disappearing into the house.

Damn, what did he think he was playing at? Meg didn't do temporary and that was all he was, no matter how tempted he'd been that night sitting in her kitchen. Besides, she had a kid and his father hadn't set the best example. *You did your best to protect your men in Afghanistan so you could learn.* Yeah, he could teach her all he knew about heavy artillery and spotting IEDs.

Rolling to his knees, he flattened his uninjured hand against the wall and slowly stood, ignoring the pain in his shoulder. At least he'd be on his feet when she got back. Yeah, like that was going to impress her after acting like a dumbass and falling through her roof.

She came back out, a small purse under her arm. "Let's get you into the truck."

"I don't need help. I can make it on my own," he grumbled but he had to admit he was hurting like a son of a bitch.

She rolled her eyes. "Uh-huh. Humor me, 'kay?"

He protested under his breath—he wasn't giving up his man card that easily—but let her guide him to the pickup, leaning more heavily on her with each step.

"Stubborn man," she said and opened the passenger door. "Do you need help getting in?"

"Of course not, but you'll have to get my keys."

"Where are they?"

"In my front pocket." A look came over her face and he had to bite back a laugh and another groan. He cleared his throat. "Left-hand side."

She drew in a breath, causing her breasts to rise under the faded T-shirt. Without another word, she stuck her hand in his pocket and fished around for the keys. Even in as much pain as he was, he couldn't help reacting to her groping fingers. He sucked in a breath.

"Sorry," she muttered and pulled out the keys, her cheeks pink. "Are you sure you don't need help getting in?"

"I got this." He used his good hand for leverage and boosted himself into the passenger seat; grateful he made it on the first try, he didn't think he had another one in him.

She slammed the door, trotted around the front and climbed in while he fumbled with his seat belt.

"Let me." She leaned over him, filling his nostrils with the scent of strawberries. She clicked the belt in place and leaned back, her hair brushing across and catching on the stubble on his chin.

"Thanks," he muttered, angry with himself because she had to help him with such a simple task as buckling his seat belt. Angrier still because his body had reacted to her. *Not a good time for this, Marine.*

He shifted in the seat and the slight movement made his ribs feel like he'd set them on fire. He swallowed hard against the nausea that roiled his stomach.

So much for being a great protector. Meg was currently the one saving his butt.

The whole trip to the hospital, Meg glanced over at him, looking for reassurance that he was still breathing. That he hadn't passed out. God, was this how he'd felt when he'd rushed her to the ER?

"Quit your fretting," he grumbled, but the lack of bite in his tone suggested he appreciated her concern.

She pulled up to the emergency entrance at the hospital and turned off the engine. "Wait right here. I'll come around and help you out," she said, sliding out and landing on the pavement with a grunt.

"I'm banged up a little, that's all," he argued.

"Humor me," she said, and then rounded the hood to his side, not at all surprised to see that he'd thrown his door open and was maneuvering his way out. Stubborn man. "Would you wait a minute? I'll get a wheelchair."

"I. Am. Walking. In." His feet hit the pavement and he stood, bent forward, leaning heavily on the door. His face paled.

Her lips pressed into a thin line. "I'm getting the chair."

He straightened slowly. His brows slammed down. "I'm walking."

Huffing out an exasperated breath, she ducked under his arm. "Fine then, but at least lean on me."

"Meggie…"

She looked up. "My mission, my rules, Marine."

He laughed. Had the gall to do so, which must've cost him, because he groaned. He let go of the door and draped his arm across her shoulders. "Don't do that. It hurts when I laugh."

She staggered under his weight, but managed to remain upright. They made their way to the entrance and through a pair of glass doors that slid open to the same small waiting area. At least the nurse manning the desk was different.

"Déjà vu all over again," Meg muttered.

"Did you not hear me when I said it hurts to laugh?" He settled in one of the seats.

"Looks like you're in a bit of pain," the nurse observed, her eyes making a quick pass over him.

"Fell through a roof," he said.

She tapped her finger on a small black pad. "Can you type your Social Security number into this for me?"

He held up his hand with its rapidly swelling wrist. "Sorry, I'm left-handed."

"I'll do it." Meg leaned forward in the seat. "Give me the info and I'll do the typing."

Meg keyed in the number as he recited it.

"Where are you hurt?" the nurse asked and they went through the same routine as before.

She knew Riley was doing his best to walk upright and under his own steam into the waiting area, but she stayed glued to his side. How long before he got to see a doctor? His eyes had drifted shut but a muscle ticked in his jaw.

As it turned out, he didn't have to wait long at all. The door to the ER buzzed open and Jan stepped through, pushing a wheelchair. His chin came up when Riley gave her what Meg guessed was his best *I'm a marine and we don't go by wheelchair* look. Obviously, Jan had encountered this a time or two in her career because she leveled him with her *I'm the one with the degree in nursing, so plant your butt in this chair* glare.

Riley mumbled under his breath and plopped himself down.

"Good choice, Marine," Jan said and smiled triumphantly.

Jan turned the wheelchair toward the door she'd come through and Meg had started to follow when Jan said, "Same rules apply. Sergeant Cooper, are you okay with Meg coming back with us?"

Riley shot her a look that said he was considering his options. Her eyes widened as she gave him an expectant gaze. "She's already seen me fall through a roof, so I guess my humiliation couldn't get much worse."

Jan barked out a laugh. "You'd be surprised."

Meg stuck her hands on her hips. "Hey, whose side are you on?"

"No fighting, ladies." Riley wiggled his eyebrows.

"As if," Meg muttered as she followed them into a small treatment room.

Jan helped him transfer from the wheelchair to a narrow stretcher. She reached into a cabinet and pulled out a hospital gown. "Seems you two can't get enough of this place."

"You gave us such good service last time," Riley told her.

"Yeah, right. Let's get you out of that shirt and get a

look at the damage," Jan said, shaking out the gown and then helping him remove his shirt. After she'd removed the shirt, she put an ice pack on his wrist.

Meg bit her lip when she saw the harsh abrasions and superficial cuts marring his flesh, the worst being over his right rib cage. The dark shadows of bruising were already setting in. A tech came in and took his vital signs while the nurse did a quick evaluation, listening to his lungs and stomach, gently probing here and there and gauging his reactions. When she finished, she draped the gown over his chest and went to the computer to document her findings.

"On a scale of zero to ten, zero being none and ten being the worst you've ever had in your life, how bad would you say your pain is?" She glanced over at him. "Be honest."

He stared at the ceiling. After a moment he said, "Six. Eight when I move or take a deep breath."

Jan nodded and added it to the chart. When she'd finished documenting, she reached for the gown. "Okay, let's get you out of those jeans so the doctor can check you over." She shook the gown out and held it up. "Can you manage or do you need help?"

He reached for the top button on his jeans, and then glanced over at Meg. "I, um…"

A phone rang. Jan pulled it out of her pocket and took the call, apologizing when she was finished. "I'm sorry. I have to take care of something, and then I'll be right back." She looked at him, at the gown, and then at Meg. "Meg, do you mind helping him change? The doctor will be in to see him in a minute."

After she'd left, Meg shuffled her feet and asked,

"Do you want me to help? Or do you want to wait for the nurse to come back?" Which scenario did *she* prefer?

"Have at it."

He would have to put it that way. They were in a hospital, for crying out loud. And he was injured. Possibly worse than either of them suspected. She swallowed hard and set her purse on the chair, taking that moment to compose herself and put on her best *I'm not thinking what I'm thinking* face.

"Okay. First I need to get those whatever-kind-of-boots they are off you."

"These are Corcoran leather jump boots."

"And you thought you'd try them out on my roof?" She closed her eyes. "Sorry. That was lame."

He *tsked*, then grinned. "I expect better from you."

"I'll try to do better next time." She knelt in front of him and untied his laces, then loosened them by tugging on the tongue. "I'll be as gentle as possible, but I think I'm going to have to pull hard to get them off."

He lifted a single eyebrow. "The last thing I want is for you to be gentle with me."

Wiggling the boot as gently as she could, she tried to ease it off but ended up having to give it a hard tug. He grunted but didn't comment. She did the same to the next one, then stood.

"Okay, now the pants."

"Now we're getting to the good stuff."

She blew out her breath. "I thought you were injured."

"Hey, I'm still a guy."

"A guy whose pants are still on."

"Sorry, just trying to lighten the mood." He scooted to the end of the stretcher and eased to his feet. "It'll make it easier if I stand."

She undid the top button and sucked in her breath at what she saw. *You've got to be kidding me.*

"Is there a problem?"

"Oh…they're button fly jeans."

"Is that a problem?"

Heck, yeah, it's a problem. It means I can't unzip and be done, quick and clean. "No."

She worked on the second button but her fingers had been replaced with sausages. *Shame on you! The man's been injured.*

"Need help down there?" The ice pack crinkled.

"No, I got it." She'd unbuttoned enough to reveal black cotton knit. Boxer briefs? Well, she'd know for sure in a moment. "Okay, let's get these off."

She stuck her thumbs through the belt loops and tugged them down past his hips. Yup. Boxer briefs. Her mouth flooded with saliva. *Really, Meg? The man is injured and you're ogling him.* She shook her head to clear it.

There were fresh bruises on his thighs. But what had her sucking in her breath were the dozens of old scars and puckered skin from burns. Her heartbeat slowed and the back of her throat burned. She reached out but her hand floundered in midair and she let it drop back down.

"Meggie?"

Chapter Seven

"Get back on the stretcher and I'll pull these off the rest of the way," she ordered in a brusque tone and squared her shoulders. How had she missed these scars that night in the motel room?

He did as she asked and she took the jeans and folded them as neatly as possible, setting them on top of the small table next to the rack of pamphlets on spotting the symptoms of strokes.

She cleared her throat, but a doctor stepping around the curtain prevented her from asking about the scars. The young doctor had a stethoscope looped around his neck and held a clipboard. He pulled a small black stool up to the stretcher, and sat down.

After introducing himself and glancing at the chart, he said, "They tell me you took the short way off the roof."

Riley huffed out a laugh, and then winced. The doctor made a note on his chart.

"You could say that," Riley said.

The doctor took down Riley's medical history and then did his evaluation. "Are you allergic to any medications?"

"No."

"I'm going to order something for pain and get pictures of those ribs and your wrist, and we'll take it from there."

After the doctor left, Meg stood up and refolded his jeans and torn T-shirt, smoothing and rearranging them on the table. Riley touched her arm and her motions stilled.

"I'm okay," he whispered.

She tucked her chin. "It's all my fault. I—"

"Stop it." He squeezed her arm. "I should have—"

A nurse stepped around the curtain.

"Okay, Sergeant Cooper, I'm going to give you an injection for pain before we get you over to Radiology." She placed a couple of syringes and two vials of medicine on the silver stand beside the stretcher and entered more information into the computer, once again asking him to verify his name and vital stats. After explaining the medications, the nurse lowered his waistband and gave him the shot in the hip. "Now…" She put a Band-Aid over the site, adjusted his gown and pulled a sheet over his hips. "Let's get you over to Radiology." She looked at Meg as she brought the rails up on the stretcher. "You can wait here, if you like. He'll be back in about ten or fifteen minutes."

Meg glanced around the room while she waited for Riley. She wrung her hands and hoped this would turn out to be one of those incidents that in time would become an amusing anecdote.

Amusing or not, she'd begun pacing by the time they wheeled Riley back. The assistant arranged the stretcher back into its original position, engaged the brake and left with a smile and a "someone will be right with you."

He reached out and grabbed her hand, pulling her close. "What's wrong?"

"How can you even ask that? I've been worried about you."

He put his arm around her and pressed her forehead against his hard, albeit bruised, chest. "I'm fine."

She pulled back to look him in the eyes. "Did they tell you that?"

"I don't need anyone to tell me how I feel." He rubbed his uninjured hand up and down her back.

"You just know it?" She wanted to hit him for sounding so cavalier. She wanted to hold him tight and soothe his injuries.

"Yup."

She heaved a sigh. "I should have called a professional roofer like you said."

"And I should have been more careful. You warned me about the part above the porch." He put a finger under her chin and forced her head up. His gaze captured hers, his voice a low rumble. "Listen to me. I know a little something about regret. Wishing you could have acted sooner or differently won't change a damn thing. All it does it eat away at your insides until there's nothing left."

He wasn't talking about falling off the roof. Was he referring to something that had happened in Afghanistan?

Talk about regrets—she had enough to last a lifetime. Why had she given up trying to reach him in Afghanistan to tell him about Fiona? Her pride would have been cold comfort if something had happened to him over there.

This wasn't the time or place to confess, but maybe she could start paving the way. But before she could say anything the doctor appeared and she stepped back. Riley dropped his arm and let her go.

The doctor glanced from one to the other and cleared his throat. "Well, good news, Sergeant Cooper. Nothing is broken. You have several bruised ribs and a minor sprain to your wrist. You'll need to wear a splint on the wrist for a couple of weeks, keep it elevated and use ice for the swelling. Ice for the ribs, as well, and periodic deep breathing to expand the lungs. No binding, though, as it hinders the deep breathing and could cause pneumonia. Your nurse will be in shortly with your splint and discharge instructions."

By the time Meg pulled up to the emergency entrance to collect her patient, Riley had mellowed from the shot for pain. Although he let the nurse know what he thought of the indignity, he sat in the wheelchair with very little fuss. He even let the two women help him get into the passenger seat.

His eyes had drifted closed before Meg exited the hospital parking lot and pulled into the late-day traffic. Thank goodness it wasn't tourist season yet, so the late-afternoon traffic was steady but not too bad. Meg was still getting used to driving his large pickup.

"I'm going to stop at the pharmacy and get your pain meds filled and I'll pick up stuff for ice packs."

"Ice packs?" He roused himself and opened one eye.

"They said you might want to ice the ribs and the wrist to help with the pain."

She ran into the pharmacy and picked up items while waiting for the prescription. Score one for small-town living.

Riley opened his eyes and attempted to sit straighter when she got back. She opened the pills and one of the bottles of water and handed them to him.

"They gave me that shot at the hospital."

"And they also said to take these to keep ahead of the pain. So do it." She shoved the bottle and pills at him.

He grumbled but took the pill and drank the water.

She started the engine and backed out of the spot. "So, how are you feeling?"

"Fine," he mumbled.

Now she knew how Riley must've felt when she was always telling him she was fine. He'd fallen asleep by the time she parked in front of her house. She ran up and opened her front door and left it standing open. Back at the truck, she opened the passenger door and squatted down. "Riley?"

She shook him.

"Huh? What?" He opened his eyes and stared at her. "Meggie? What're you doing here?"

"I live here."

He glanced around and frowned. "The roof…"

"Yes, you fell. Remember?" She reached over and undid his seat belt. "We should get you inside."

"Mmm…strawberries." He sniffed her. "Did I ever tell you how much I like your hair?"

"You used to make fun of it." She lifted his legs out. "Here, lean on me."

"Where we goin'?" He slid out of the truck.

"I need to get you into bed."

"It's about time." He reached for her but swayed and had to lean against the truck. "Been dreamin' 'bout you... Do you dream about me?"

More than you'll ever know. "Uh-huh. Now, let's get you inside."

"Did you miss me, Meggie, 'cause I sure missed you."

"You did?" She stumbled and was surprised they both didn't end up face-first in the gravel.

"I messed up." He shook his head. "So many times. Sweet Meggie, so many."

"What?"

"What?" he mimicked and looked at her, his eyes not quite focused.

Her heart pounded in her chest and she had trouble breathing, but she asked, "What did you mess up?"

"Huh?" He scowled. "I...don't...but it was bad."

She stopped and he bumped against her. Was he talking about returning her letters or something else, something that was causing his nightmare?

"Meggie? I...need to...lie down."

"Okay, but let's get you inside first."

Slowly they made their way onto the porch.

"Meggie?"

"What?" She pushed the door open wider.

"S-sorry I broke your pretty chair."

She glanced at the pile of wood that used to be her Adirondack chair. "I'm just glad you're okay."

Inside, she helped him over to the couch. "I'm going to go and get Liam's old room ready. I think it's best if you stay here until you have use of both hands again."

Before going to bed that night, she checked on him, but he was snoring softly. She got the night-light from

Fiona's room and plugged it into an outlet next to the bed. She set a bottle of water on the nightstand along with his bottle of painkillers and smoothed out the blanket, her gaze lingering on his sleeping form. She couldn't prevent her fingers from running ever so lightly down his cheek. He'd said earlier that he'd messed up and she desperately wanted to believe he'd been talking about not contacting her after he deployed, but she was afraid. Afraid to hope for something that wouldn't happen once she told him the truth about Fiona. He'd hate her and she wouldn't blame him. Turning on her heel, she left and went to her own room.

After washing up and brushing her teeth, she changed into her soft flannel nightshirt. It might be May but the evenings were still cool. She pulled back the covers and crawled between the sheets. Without Fiona the house lacked warmth. Hugging the extra pillow to her chest, she finally drifted off to sleep.

She awoke with a start. At first she wasn't sure what had woken her, and then realized she'd heard the toilet flush. Riley. She threw off the covers and rushed into the hall.

He was coming out of the bathroom. Although it was dark in the hall, light spilled out from the night-lights in the bathroom and guest room. Enough light for her to see he was—oh, dear Lord! He was naked. She shouldn't look. Really, she— Oh, how could she not?

"Sorry if I woke you." He propped himself against the door frame.

"That's okay... I... I..." She tried to swallow but her tongue scratched like sandpaper over the roof of her mouth. "Did you know you're…naked?" Her voice rose on that last word.

"Nothing slips past you."

"Why?" she managed before clamping her mouth shut. Adult women did not giggle hysterically at the sight of a naked man.

"Why what?"

She grabbed her elbows to keep from reaching for him, to keep from running her hands over that splendid male body. "Huh?"

He straightened, pulling away from the door frame, and the light, no longer blocked by his body, spilled into the hallway and onto him. "You asked me why."

"I… I did?"

"You did." He stalked toward her. "I'm going to assume you were asking why I took off my skivvies. I got tired of fumbling with one hand and tore them off."

She took a step back and tried not to stare—no, really, she did try. But her gaze zeroed in on a particular part of his anatomy. The part that rose a little with each step he took.

"Is that what you were asking me, Meg?"

"I… I… Uh." How the hell she managed to look him in the face, she couldn't say. "Did…uh, did you need anything?"

"As a matter of fact, I do."

Me? Please, please let it be me. "W-what did you need?"

"A glass of water to take another pain pill."

"Oh." Disappointment laced her tone. What had she been expecting? Declarations of undying love? At this point, she was willing for a declaration of good, old-fashioned lust. She cleared her throat before saying, "I thought I'd left a bottle of water on the nightstand."

"You did." He held up his sprained hand. "I was having trouble getting it open."

She drew her brows together. It was taking all of her willpower to keep meeting his gaze instead of looking down, and the effort was affecting her mental capabilities. "Oh… Oh! Geez, how could I have been so stupid? Let me get you a glass."

"No need. Open the bottle for me. We can leave the cap off."

"Oh…sure." She clamored into his room. She'd go open his water bottle, leave the cap off and then go straight back to bed. *Do not pass Go. Do not collect two hundred dollars. And do not, under any circumstances, do not look at his—*

"If you keep squeezing it like that, there won't be any water left." He reached around her and tugged the bottle from her hand. He threw a pill into his mouth and took a sip of the water and set it back down.

"Oh… I…well…" She wiped her hands on her sleepshirt and ignored the puddle at her feet. "I better just… and—"

"Lie down with me." He stood close and danced his fingertips over the back of her neck. Leaning down, he whispered, "I want to feel you next to me. Please."

His breath caressed her cheek and blew the hair around her ear, melting her defenses. "I don't want to hurt your ribs or your wrist."

"You won't." He placed a light kiss on her temple. "My left side is the worst. You can sleep on the right."

She sighed and he urged her closer, cajoling, "You know you want to."

She did. God help her, she did. He pulled the covers back and slipped into the bed, patting the empty spot next to him. She called herself all kinds of a fool, but followed him into the bed. He put his arm around her and she snuggled up against his side, enjoying the solid warmth next to her. She luxuriated in the feeling of belonging, of feeling secure. *Watch out. Don't get used to it.* Riley was returning to Afghanistan. Meg McBride wasn't enough to hold a man like Riley Cooper in a Podunk little town like Loon Lake.

He rested his cheek against her hair and she snuggled closer. "I shouldn't have disappeared on you, but I needed to clear my head before the funeral."

"You could've said something. I would have understood." She splayed her fingers over his heart. "I can't begin to imagine what it must be like trying to make that transition, but I can respect your need for space."

"Can you forgive me?"

"Always." She ran her fingers through the fine hairs on his chest.

He yawned and she struggled to sit up, but he held her tight.

"You need to rest."

"I can do that better with you here…beside me." His hand caressed her neck and shoulder, where he had placed his arm around her.

The callus on his thumb sent shivers of awareness shooting through her. "Are the painkillers working?"

"Mmm, they've taken the edge off. The abrasions aren't anything compared to shrapnel."

"The scars on your legs?"

"And other places."

"What happened?"

She waited, but when he remained silent, she sighed and figured he didn't want to talk about it. She needed to respect that. Laying her hand against his side, she said, "You don't have to tell me."

"I want to but it's…it's not easy. There's a lot I don't even remember. Those are the parts I have nightmares about."

She remained silent, ready to listen to whatever he had to tell her. Maybe if she knew what had happened to him over there, she'd have a better understanding of him, who he was now.

He blew out his breath. "I learned that even the most insignificant decisions could have deadly consequences."

She shifted closer to him. "I know you, Riley Cooper. I'm sure you always did the best you could."

He gave a mirthless laugh. "Tell that to PFC Alex Trejo's parents. Their only child came home in a flag-draped coffin."

"Tell me what happened. Sometimes it helps to get things out in the open." She had no right to say something like that. No right at all. She was holding on to one of the biggest secrets ever. But right now this was about Riley and if talking about something would help him, she needed to listen.

"We were ordered to clear a village of insurgents. That meant going from building to building and checking. We went into a school… There…there were still children inside." He swallowed hard. "We thought we'd gotten them all, when one of them told us there were still three children on the third floor. I ordered Trejo to come with me and we went up but couldn't find anyone. We were egressing. The others had already moved on… I was first to reach the stairs but the stench was bad in that place and it was hot… The sweat was getting in my eyes and I paused to wipe them… He got ahead of me… made some smart-ass comment…"

She dropped featherlight kisses on his shoulder and waited for him to continue.

"I don't even remember what he said or what I said in return…it was just trash talk…a coping mechanism. God, why can't I remember the last thing I said to him…?"

He drew in a breath and continued, "I didn't know it at the time but learned later someone lobbed an M-67 Frag at us—that's a fragmentation grenade."

"The shrapnel scars on your legs?"

His chin brushed her temple when he nodded and he swallowed before continuing. "Trejo, a kid with his whole life ahead of him, shoved me back and slammed the door in my face. I remember being pissed…then nothing."

"What happened?" she whispered, afraid to break the spell and have him shut her out again.

"He spotted it first and dove onto the damn thing." He sighed, his breath disturbing her hair. "He had the presence of mind to slam the door or I would have died, too."

She clamped her mouth over the words that wanted to come out. He wouldn't want to hear them. And she didn't want them to sound like pity. He wouldn't appreciate that coming from her. And she didn't pity him.

She was sorry for what he'd had to go through but not for the man that he was.

"He…he sacrificed himself to save my sorry ass… I shouldn't have let anything stop me from leading the way. Trejo had a family to go home to…a family he was homesick for…a real family that wanted him." He sucked in a shaky breath. "I was in charge. I should have gone down those stairs first. That's what a leader does."

His words about family shredded her heart like confetti. *I want you… I've always wanted you*, she screamed inside her head. The expression on his face told her he wasn't in a place to hear that from her. And she didn't want to stop him. He needed to get his story out so he could begin to heal.

Still, she needed to comfort him, so she did the only thing she knew. She held him and listened.

"*Christ*, Meggie, I can hear him screaming." He made a strangled, choking sound. "They told me he was killed instantly, but I can hear him in my head…you know?"

She didn't say anything, but hugged him tighter, rained kisses on his chest and shoulder.

"I should have gone down those stairs first," he repeated and made another choking sound.

"Why?" When he didn't respond she continued, "Don't diminish his act by feeling responsible or by not thinking you deserve to survive as much as the next man."

"You sound like that counselor they sent me to."

"Doctor Meg, that's me." She'd tried for a light tone but knew she'd failed.

She kissed his cheek and would have pulled away but his arms clamped around her, crushing her to him. He buried his face in her hair, whispering her name over and over. His lips found hers and pressed. His kiss was desperate, as if he was searching for salvation. And she'd give it to him. Tonight was all that mattered. This night. This man. She kissed him back with her own hungry need. She didn't realize how close she and Fiona had come to losing him forever. She knew that once she told him about Fiona she might still lose him. He might not ever forgive her. But she needed this, needed one more night, one that might have to last her the rest of her life. She knew now that she would never love any man the way she loved Riley. Her mom had claimed the women in her family loved but once and neither time nor distance extinguished it.

He ran his fingers over her thighs and around her hip. "You have a lot more curves now. So sexy. So beautiful."

She arched her head back as he nibbled on her earlobe, and ran his tongue along the spot under her ear.

When she moaned, he smiled against her damp skin. "I remember how much you liked that."

"Yes," she murmured, lost in the sensations he was creating.

"I've never wanted another woman like I've wanted you," he said hoarsely. "Do you want me, Meggie?"

"Yes…only you…only you."

He groaned and his leg pushed her thighs open. His tongue pressed against the seam of her lips, demanding entry. She opened her mouth and his tongue thrust in, dueling with hers. All thoughts flew out of her head. Sensation ruled.

His hand slid between her legs and found the spot begging for attention, but only skimmed it and instead pushed into her folds.

"Riley..." she groaned.

He slid his finger out to tease her, then increased the pressure, finding a rhythm that had her heels digging into the soft cotton sheets. The tension coiled low in her stomach, making her feet scrape against the mattress.

Just when she thought she couldn't take any more, she unraveled as if Riley had pulled a knot that she hadn't even realized was so tight.

Chapter Eight

She lay pressed against his chest, feeling his rapidly beating heart beneath her. When she started to sit up, he put his hand behind her head and brought her face down and kissed her.

"Sweet, sweet, Meggie," he whispered against her lips.

"It's been so long," he told her.

"Too long. Please, I... I..."

"Tell me what you want," he murmured.

"You. I want you."

"Baby, you'll have to get on top."

"I don't want to hurt your ribs," she panted.

"You won't... God, Meggie, I need you." He nipped the crook of her neck, then trailed his tongue across the spot.

She climbed on top of him, and his hands guided her knees closer to his waist.

His arousal pressed against her stomach. She reached down to touch it and his hips bucked toward her. He pushed her nightshirt up. She let go of him so she could lift her arms to get the garment over her head. She leaned over him, and his mouth traced a path down her throat to her breasts, his tongue leaving a moist trail and delicious goose bumps on her sensitive skin. His mouth found her nipple. First, he licked, and then blew on the crested peak, driving her mad with need. When she whispered a plea, he drew it into his mouth and sucked on it. Her body flamed with yearning. She couldn't imagine allowing any other man to touch her the way Riley did.

His mouth left that nipple and his tongue drew a path across the valley of her breasts to the other one. He latched on and she cried out in pleasure. Riley was making love to her. She had longed for this moment, for him.

His hand found her panties and slipped inside. His palm cupped her, then he slipped a finger inside her while his thumb stroked her nub. All her nerve endings hummed and sizzled as his callused finger and thumb drove her to the edge.

She cried out in frustration when he pulled his hand away.

"Riley, please," she sobbed and arched herself toward him.

He tugged on her purple bikinis. "I used to dream of this while I was over there…night after night."

She helped him get her panties off and tossed them aside; he urged her higher up his chest, whispering, "I want to taste you."

Spreading her legs, he licked the sensitive flesh on her inner thighs. She shook her head and cried in frustration. She grabbed his head between her hands and tried to guide his head to the part of her that ached for his touch. When his mouth finally found that spot, she cried out and dug her fingers into his scalp.

"Riley, please," she begged again.

But he had other ideas and he controlled the pace, bringing her to the edge, then easing up.

When he pulled away, she whimpered. "Riley?"

"I need my wallet," he muttered and glanced around the dimly lit room.

"Wallet? Now? Why?"

"Condoms…unless you're on the pill?"

She shook her head. "No pill. No need. There hasn't been anyone since…since I had Fiona."

He cupped her face with his good hand and kissed her. "Sweet, sweet, Meggie."

"I remember seeing it on the dresser." She untangled herself from him, careful not to hurt his injuries, and darted across the cool wooden floor. Grabbing the wallet, she brought it back and handed it to him. He reached in and pulled out a condom.

He held out the small square packet. "I'm at a disadvantage with only one good hand."

She took it and tried to rip the foil. It wouldn't budge. She tried again but her fingers were slick and wouldn't cooperate.

"Meggie?"

"I can't get it open." She shook her head and bit her lower lip.

"We'll figure something out." He pulled her close to his side and kissed her temple. "How about if you hold it and I'll give it a tug with my good hand?"

She lifted on her elbow. "But…won't that…hurt?"

"I meant the condom wrapper," he said.

"I… I knew that," she sputtered, and even after all they'd done, she knew her face was red.

"Liar." He brushed the hair away from her face and rubbed his thumb along her lower lip.

Working together, they got the stubborn wrapper open.

"Careful, or this won't last very long," he cautioned and handed her the condom.

She rolled it down his impressive length. "I want you inside me."

He huffed out a laugh. "That's the plan."

She scooted onto the bed. He dipped his fingers into her and brought her back to the peak in a few short strokes. She positioned herself over him and lowered herself so the head was inside.

"So tight," he said through gritted teeth as if he was using all his willpower not to pull her completely down on top of him.

"Like I said, it's been a while." She brought him close to her, teasing and testing.

"Oh, God, Meggie," he groaned. "It feels so good."

"That's the plan." She parroted his earlier words and laughed, warmth radiating through her entire body.

His groans made her heart rate jump and her breathing increase. Last time they made love he'd been in charge and she'd enjoyed it…but now she loved being in charge.

He urged her down with his hand on her hip. He filled her up but then she lifted to draw him back out. She wasn't ready for this to end yet and increased the pace only to slow it down again.

"Such a tease," he muttered through clenched teeth

and teased her by gently squeezing first one nipple, then the other.

The sensations began to build past the point where she could continue teasing. She writhed as the pressure built, her blood pounded and her heart raced. "Riley, I…"

"Show me, Meggie—show me what you want."

Her fingers dug into the sprinkling of hairs on his chest. Her hips gyrated as she reached for it but couldn't quite reach it. She sobbed in frustration. "Please…"

"Here, baby…let me help you." He used his finger to bring her over the edge.

Her world exploded for the second time that night, but she realized she hadn't taken Riley with her. She began riding him again, intent upon making their night as unforgettable for him as it would be for her.

"Yes…like that," he groaned and cupped his hands around her bottom.

His hips rose to meet and guide her movements until he shouted, finding his own release.

Sated and spent she lay on top of him for a few moments. When she started to sit up, he put his hand behind her head and brought her face down and kissed her.

"Sweet, sweet, Meggie," he whispered against her lips. "I need to take care of the condom."

"Of course." She would've left the bed but he stopped her with a hand on her arm.

"Stay," he growled.

"Woof," she said and he bared his teeth at her before going into the bathroom, sending her into a fit of the giggles.

She was still grinning when he returned and slipped into bed beside her and pulled the covers around them. He tucked her close and she snuggled against him.

"That was—" A yawn cut her off.

She felt him smile against her hair.

"It was," he agreed and rested his cheek against the top of her head.

She drifted off, but woke when he stirred, probably seeking a more comfortable position.

Raising herself onto an elbow, she asked, "Do you need more painkillers?"

"Nah, I'm okay."

"Are you sure? You don't have to be all macho on my account."

He laughed and his warm breath disturbed the hair over her ear. "I wouldn't dream of it."

"I promise I won't think less of you. I already know you're a badass marine and all." She'd done her best to keep her tone light, but she heard the catch in her voice at the end.

"Is that what you think?"

"It's what I know." She shrugged one shoulder, even though she knew he couldn't see her motion in the dark. "Why does it mean so much to you?"

He was silent for so long, she assumed he wasn't going to answer. Sighing, she started to move away so he could get comfortable, but he pulled her back.

"Careful. Don't hurt yourself," she said.

"Please, Meggie, don't pull away."

She settled back against him, but kept silent.

"I like the structure, the stability."

"I'm not sure I understand," she whispered.

"You knew about my parents' divorce?"

"Yes."

He sighed. "I thought once they separated, things

would get better. They'd go their separate ways and the constant fighting would stop."

"It didn't?"

"Hell, their marriage was contentious, but the divorce was worse. And I was stuck in the middle…expected to be a tattletale. And used as a weapon against the other when I wasn't ignored."

Meg's eyes burned and her throat clogged, but she managed to say, "I'm sorry. I had no idea."

"You were young. And I spent time with your family to get away, to forget what waited for me at home. I didn't want to bring it with me."

Without another word, she began kissing each one of his visible scars, wishing she could kiss the invisible ones, too. She refused to regret what they'd done. Even if Riley left tomorrow, she wasn't going to regret grabbing this little bit of heaven.

Riley awoke and tried to move. Had he been run over by a tank? What else would explain the aches and stiffness? He couldn't be in a hospital because he was naked and something warm snuggled up against him. *Meggie.* And she was naked, too.

She shifted and opened her eyes. "Hey."

He wanted to pull a victory fist pump but figured she wouldn't appreciate the purely male gesture.

"Hey, yourself."

She stretched and yawned. "How are you feeling this morning?"

"Other than not being able to move without almost every inch of my body screaming in protest, I feel great."

"Oh. Well, I'd better get up. I—"

He reached for her. "Not so fast. I said *almost* every inch... There are still inches that are working fine. And if I could move I'd prove it to you."

"And those are mighty impressive inches." She began kissing her way down his chest. "Maybe I can help."

Oh, yeah, he could definitely get used to waking up next to Meggie. He hadn't thought he wanted marriage or family, but this time spent with her had him reevaluating his long-term plans. He liked being a part of her life. Even falling off the damn roof had a silver lining.

His thoughts dissolved into a haze of pleasure as Meggie's lips, mouth and tongue continued to work their way toward their final destination. Yes, please let that be her intention.

Having Meggie snuggled next to him every night and every morning would be a pleasure he could get used to. Imagine the fun they could have once his injuries healed.

She lifted her head and he groaned. What a tease; she was killing him. "Meggie, I—"

"Ssshh. Did you hear that?"

"What?" He lifted his head off the pillow. He'd been lost in a haze of pleasure, his battle-honed instincts shut off. Levering himself onto his elbow, he listened, and there was the distinctive sound of a diesel engine in the driveway. Who in the world?

"That." Meg slid off the bed and went to the window. She cracked the blinds and looked out while he admired her bare backside. "Oh. My. God."

Swearing and clutching his ribs, Riley scrambled to a sitting position and swung his legs over the side of the bed. "What is it?"

She looked over her shoulder, her face pale. "It's my dad and Fiona. They weren't due back until the weekend."

Still naked, she trotted over to the door, muttering under her breath. "Not good. So not good."

"Hey, wait."

"What? I haven't got time for—"

"You're not going to greet them naked, are you?"

She swore. "I need to get dressed. So do you. Quick."

He held up his brace. "Nothing's gonna happen fast, sweetheart."

"Damn." She turned back and scooped up his jeans from the floor. "Let's get these on you."

He shoved his feet into the legs of the worn denim and winced, thinking about trying to stuff himself into the pants. Talk about timing. Ten more minutes and he'd have been a happy, limp camper.

Easing off the bed, he stood while Meg tugged his pants up. By the time she reached critical mass, her face was as red as the fire truck Mac used to drive. He welcomed seeing Mac again, but he wished the conditions were anything but this.

"Riley?" She chewed on her bottom lip.

"Yeah." He sighed and used his good hand to try to stuff himself into the jeans, but even his good hand was weak due to the pain in his shoulder.

"Here, let me," she said as she took him in hand and attempted to guide him into the pants.

His hips bucked as if they were no longer under his command and he bit back a groan. "You're killing me."

She dropped her hand and jumped back. "Did I hurt you?"

"Let's just say it's a good kind of pain."

"Well, I—"

A door slammed.

"Christ, you standing naked in front of me isn't help-ing." He made a shooing motion with his hand. "Get dressed. I'll take care of this."

In her own room, Meg grabbed yesterday's sweatshirt and jeans from the chair by her bed and tried to get them on, but her hands were shaking so hard they hindered her. What if they'd come back early because something was wrong with Fiona? Oh, God. And here she was be-having like a stupid, hormone-crazed teen again. Jump-ing into bed with Riley after being together with him for like ten minutes was a stupid, stupid thing to do. She should have been listening to her head.

She stopped at Riley's door and glanced in. He was struggling with his T-shirt. She ran in and helped pull it over his head.

"Thanks," he said when his head popped out of the neck hole.

She nodded and left. "I'll be outside."

She unlocked and opened the front door. Her dad stood on the porch looking up at the damage. His dark hair was liberally sprinkled with gray, but to Meg he looked younger than he had in the past several years. Guilt jabbed her in the gut for not being as happy as she should have been in the beginning about him find-ing a new love.

Mac noticed her and pointed to the gaping, jagged hole and the remains of the broken wooden chair. "Are you okay?"

"I'm fine." He pulled her into a tight embrace and she kissed his cheek before stepping away. "Welcome back."

"What the hell happened?"

"It's a long story."

"You're sure you're okay?" He sounded doubtful and looked her up and down as if expecting to see bruises.

She forced a laugh and spread her arms to show him she was unharmed. "I'm not hurt."

He rubbed a hand over his mouth. "I knew this place was going to be too much for you. Wicked expensive to heat. Not to mention the—"

"Where are Fiona and Doris?"

He flicked his thumb toward the motor home. "They're getting dressed. They were still asleep when we pulled in. I drove all night."

"Why? Is everything okay?" Her heart began to beat faster and she latched onto his arm.

"Yeah, we're good. We left ahead of schedule to try to get a jump on the road closures due to smoke from those wildfires in Utah."

Letting her breath out, she squeezed his arm. "You mean you didn't try to volunteer to help fight them?"

Mac grinned sheepishly. "Doris threatened me with bodily harm."

"Ah, so she knows you."

"You got that right. You gonna tell me what happened here?"

She would have to admit to her harebrained scheme to patch the leaky roof. She could imagine what he'd have to say about that. Not to mention getting to hear again all the reasons why moving here was a bad idea. "I'll explain but first I want to see Fiona. Please. It feels like forever since I kissed my baby. She's probably grown while you were gone."

"Go see her. I don't think this hole is going anywhere."

Meg leaned over and kissed her dad's cheek. "Love you, Pop."

She was delaying the inevitable, but she hurried to the motor home. Maybe she'd come up with a reasonable explanation, one that didn't make her look foolish for trying to fix her own roof. Yeah, like that was gonna happen. She opened the door to the camper, calling out hello as she did.

Riley stepped onto the porch in time to see Meg disappear into the huge Class A motor home, but he'd heard enough of the exchange between her and her dad. Was Meg avoiding telling her dad the truth because she didn't want Mac knowing he'd been helping? Or did she not want to admit she might be in over her head? Once his wrist and ribs healed, he could help her knock out some of the repairs on this place. Damn, what was he thinking?

Mac McBride was staring up at the hole, scratching his head. "How the hell...?"

"That's my fault, sir." Riley came through the door and sauntered onto the porch. The aglets from the laces of his untied boots made clicking noises on the wooden floor of the porch. "Entirely my fault."

"Riley Cooper?" Mac took a step forward and stuck out his hand. "I didn't know you were here. It's been ages. How are you, son?"

Riley held up his hand with the removable cast. "I've been better, sir."

"What happened?"

Mac seemed pleased to see him and Riley relaxed. "I was trying to help Meg. I noticed worn shingles and thought I could help out some before she got a roofer."

"The hell you say?"

Riley shrugged and winced at the pain, but was determined not to cause any trouble between Meg and her dad. "Meg tried to warn me there might be weak spots over the porch, but…"

Mac shook his head, his face grim. "I was worried this place would be too much for her. Especially since I didn't keep up the maintenance like I should have. That part's on me."

"Well, that—" Riley pointed his plastered hand toward the gaping hole "—is on me, sir. She's done a helluva job with repairs and renovations."

"That so?"

"I can tell how much she loves this place." Riley knew that much and, truth be told, he was proud of her. His gut clenched and he suddenly wished he could be "that guy" for Meg, sitting in her cheerful kitchen watching her make supper, but his future was in a tent or a mine-resistant armored personnel carrier with his men.

He never should have touched, tasted, wanted—then or now. What a dumbass he'd been, thinking he could have Meg once more and not crave her and what she represented for the rest of his life.

The door to the motor home opened and a little girl—make that a miniature Meg—hopped down the steps, pigtails bouncing as if she were a puppet. Her eyes wide behind pink wire-rimmed glasses, she made a beeline toward the porch, her sneakers crunching and scattering the gravel in the driveway. The girl was definitely a mini-Meg, right down to the red corkscrew curls. Riley's throat closed and he had to stiffen his knees to remain upright. He'd never seen himself as a father, but the idea held a certain appeal. Damn, where did that crazy thought come from?

Despite the pain in his ribs and thighs, he squatted so he was eye level with the kid. "Hello, there. I'm Riley. Who are you?"

Chapter Nine

"I'm Fee-oh-nah…like the princess." She planted her hands on her hips and stuck one foot out. "Mrs. Grampa Mac bought me new sneakers at the giant mall 'cuz my old ones pinched me. She let me pick them out and when Grampa Mac told us to hurry she said, 'Tim, you hush up,' and told me I could take as long as I wanted." She giggled, her bony shoulders going up and down. "Tim. That's what she calls my Grampa Mac."

Riley sucked in a quick breath, searching for something to say to the little dynamo. He'd never been one for kids, but something in his chest expanded and he was fascinated. He put it down to her looking so much like Meg. *Yeah, you tell yourself that if it helps.* "I see."

She jiggled her foot, setting off a light show in the soles of the sneakers. "They're pink. These ones have lights. See? Grampa Mac says I don't need lights on my shoes 'cuz everyone hears me coming."

"I can believe that." Riley blew out his breath. Nothing shy about this kid. His gut clenched at the thought of staying here...being a part of both her and Meg's lives.

Her brow wrinkled, and she pointed to his arm. "How did you get hurt, Mr. Riley?"

"See that hole? I fell through." He tried to inhale but his chest hurt. If he had stayed with Meg instead of joining the marines, all this might have been his: the sunny kitchen, the little chatterbox and Meg.

Her gaze followed to where he was pointing. "Gee, Mr. Riley, maybe you'd better not do that no more."

The tightness in his chest eased and he grinned. "Believe me, I won't."

Fiona glanced toward the camper and back. "Did Mommy yell at you for making a hole?"

Riley winked at her. "No, she was very nice about it and took me to the hospital."

The girl nodded. "Yeah, she's good like that."

Meg came out of the camper, followed by an attractive woman with dark hair and sparkling eyes. Riley guessed the woman to be in her late fifties like Mac, and he could see why Mac was smitten.

When Fiona ran to her mother, Riley rose. His stupid heart flip-flopped like a landed fish when Meg picked up the little girl and nuzzled her neck, making Fiona giggle. Just as he had when he was growing up, Riley envied what the McBrides shared. Despite his close friendship with Liam and the family's welcoming nature, Riley had always felt like an outsider, as if their family dynamics had been making a mockery of his reality. He'd found is place in the world, with his men, antitank fire in-
of a child's laughter, the smell of death instead of

home-cooked meals and his rifle to keep him company at night instead of Meg.

The older woman approached him and smiled. "Hello. You must be Riley."

"Yes, ma'am."

She lifted her eyebrows. "Ma'am?"

Mac laughed. "Cut him some slack, Doris. He's a marine."

"Well, in that case, he's forgiven." She winked at Riley and went to Mac's side. Mac put his arm around her waist; she leaned into him and he kissed her temple.

Oh, yeah, Mac was a goner.

Riley's gaze went to Meg, and he wished he had the right to touch Meg the way Mac did Doris, but despite the passion they'd shared last night, Meg wasn't his. This morning had brought that fact home more than anything.

"If you hadn't guessed it by now, this is my wife, Doris," Mac said.

Doris glanced from the hole to his arm. "You take a shortcut?"

"Something like that." Riley turned toward Meg. "I was telling your dad how I saw some bad spots in your roof and got careless."

Meg opened her mouth and shut it again without speaking. She met his gaze, and her eyes softened; he answered the warming light with a slight nod.

Doris squeezed Mac's arm. "Tim, can't you do something to help?"

Mac smiled at his wife. "A couple of guys in my former firehouse do roofing on the side. I'll talk to them."

Riley nodded. "I feel responsible, so let me know how much, sir."

Meg stepped forward. "Pop, that's not nece—"

"I'm sure we can work something out. Those guys owe me a few favors," Mac said and pulled out his cell phone.

"Have you had breakfast yet?" Meg set Fiona on the ground. "I was about to make some pancakes."

"I'll help," said Doris. She reached her hand out to Fiona. "Why don't we go help your mommy?"

In the kitchen Meg tried to control the trembling in her hands as she got out the ingredients for breakfast. She'd already planned on making breakfast for Riley, albeit much later. Her cheeks burned and her heart pounded at the thought of her dad and Doris almost catching them. Yeah, repeating past mistakes was not how she wanted to greet her dad. Liam had guessed from the start that Riley was Fiona's father, but as far as Meg knew, her dad had no clue.

"Mommy?" Fiona tugged on Meg's sleeve. "Can I go to my room and check on my aminals? I missed them while I was gone on a bacation."

"Sure, sweetie. I assure you they're all still there and I imagine they missed you, too."

Fiona danced around on her toes. "Then can I go help Grampa Mac and Mr. Riley look at the hole?"

"Okay, but don't get in the way," Meg instructed.

"I won't," she said as she skipped to her room.

When they were alone, Meg cleared her throat and asked, "How much do I owe you for Fiona's sneakers? I didn't plan for you to have to buy her new ones."

Doris waved her hand in a dismissive gesture. "It was my pleasure. I had fun shopping with her."

Meg cracked eggs into a vintage batter bowl with pink e stripes. "Even if my dad told you to hurry?"

Doris laughed. "I could see Fiona getting nervous and I didn't want her to have to make a rushed choice to please the adults."

"Thank you for that." Meg beat the eggs. "And…and thank you for giving her an exciting vacation."

Measuring the dry ingredients, the older woman said, "When Jake and Wayne were both killed by that drunk driver, I not only lost a husband and son, but any hope I had of having grandchildren. So it's been a dream come true spending time with Fiona, even if she calls me Mrs. Grampa Mac."

"I can speak to her and—"

Doris reached over and touched Meg's arm. "It doesn't matter what she calls me. I'm having too much fun spoiling a grandchild to care if I'm grandma or Mrs. Grandma. She's such a sweet little girl."

"Thanks." Meg gave her a quick hug. "It's been nice for Fiona to have a grandmother."

Doris greased the electric griddle Meg had gotten out. "I hope you were able to accomplish a lot without your little helper."

You have no idea. "Not as much as I'd hoped."

"How long has Riley been here?" Doris asked in a neutral tone.

Meg sighed. "He's renting the cottage next door."

"I'm not judging, dear." Doris plugged in the griddle. "You're a grown woman."

Meg mixed the batter with a bit too much gusto. "Who also happens to be a single mother in a very small town."

"But everyone in Loon Lake loves and admires you."

Meg pushed the bowl away before she mixed the batter too much. "Not as much as they love to gossip. I don't want Fiona hurt."

"Oh, I'm sure it's not that bad. You're a wonderful mother and everyone knows it." Doris gave a discreet cough. "And you can't expect someone like your Riley Cooper to go unnoticed."

"He's not my anything," Meg said, but after last night, her assertion had lost its vehemence. She sighed and her shoulders drooped. "He's not staying. He'll be gone as soon as his leave is up."

"What about Fiona?" Doris set a platter next to the griddle. "Surely he wants to be a part of her life."

"You know?" Meg's jaw dropped. "But…how?"

Doris gently squeezed her arm. "Anyone seeing them together would suspect. And observing your nervousness clinched it for me."

"That obvious, huh?"

"I'm afraid so." Doris nodded.

Meg plopped scoopfuls of batter onto the griddle. "I'm sure he'll want to be involved once he finds out."

"Good Lord, you mean he doesn't know?" Doris shook her head. "It's none of my business, but these things have a way of coming out anyway. And it's hard not to miss, dear. There's a striking resemblance."

Meg had always considered the resemblance between Fiona and Riley to be obvious, but she wasn't sure if that was all in her head. Doris confirmed it wasn't. "I'm trying to figure out how. Liam knows, but I swore him to secrecy. Do you think my dad suspects at all?"

Doris glanced out the window. "I have to assume Tim hasn't put two and two together yet. Riley's still in one piece out there. Huh, I always thought Fiona looked like you until I saw them together."

"I know. Mini Cooper, right?"

Doris laughed. "If you'd like, I can suggest Tim and I take Fiona for a walk down by the lake before we leave."

"Thanks." Meg flipped the first batch of pancakes. "That would help. I don't know what his reaction will be and I wouldn't want Fiona around."

"That might be best. We can keep her occupied for a bit longer."

"Thanks." Meg slipped the pancakes onto the waiting platter. "I hate to disappoint Dad yet again when he finds out."

Doris tilted her head. "Disappoint your dad? Whatever do you mean, dear?"

Staring down at her feet, Meg tried to swallow the lump in her throat. "I know how much I disappointed him when I got pregnant at nineteen and then dropped out of college."

"I can assure you, Meg, you did not disappoint him." Doris laid a comforting hand on her back. "He's told me over and over how proud he is of you, how hard you've worked to finish your education and what a wonderful mother you are."

Meg blinked against the burning in the back of her eyes. "Really?"

Doris rubbed Meg's shoulder blades. "Yes, of course."

Meg sniffed. "But…"

"If anything, he's upset with himself. He'd told me more than once how he let you down when your mom died. I know he fell apart and you stepped up." She shook her head. "Instead of letting you lean on him when you lost your mother, Tim said both he and Liam leaned on you and he admired how strong you are."

Meg flipped the last batch of pancakes. "But…he never…"

Doris set the silverware next to the plates. "Of course he didn't. Tim—your dad—is pretty old school, in case you hadn't noticed."

"But he told you." Meg winced. She sounded like Fiona when she whined about fairness.

"Because he knew I wouldn't get all emotional when he did. He could say it in a very matter-of-fact way."

"Yeah, when you put it like that." Meg set the platter of pancakes on the table as the tension knotting her stomach relaxed. "Better let them know breakfast is ready."

Meg's stomach knotted again when Fiona insisted on sitting next to Riley. Her dad was watching the two of them, seated side by side, and the resemblance was unmistakable.

After studying the two of them, her dad turned to Doris. A silent communication passed between them and when he turned back to Riley, his eyebrows crashed together and his expression turned grim.

Meg's stomach rolled. Surely, her dad knew better than to say anything in front of Fiona. Thank goodness her daughter was too excited about being home to pick up on the sudden tension.

Riley glanced around the table at the others, sensing the sudden tension. He'd attempted to gain Meg's attention, but she refused to make eye contact. This had nothing to do with their spending the night together. He was sure of it, despite that being the most obvious explanation of her avoiding looking at him.

"Mr. Riley?"

He turned his attention to Fiona. She was looking at

him with eyes the same shade of gray as his. But that wasn't possible. Meg would never do that to him. Sweat beaded above his upper lip. And if someone had asked him, he would've sworn he'd never do something as shameful as abandoning the mother of his child.

Thoughts whirled around in his head until it felt as though that frag grenade had exploded inside his skull. He rubbed his temple, trying to ease the ache.

"Mr. Riley? Can you pour my syrup? It comes out too fast." She leaned closer. "Mommy says I'm not 'sposed to drown the pancakes."

As if on autopilot, he managed to smile and pour the correct amount of syrup. His heart stuttered when she smiled her appreciation and he knew he would fight to his last breath to protect this child.

My God, was it possible? Could this precious little girl be his? His and Meg's? But, no, Meg wouldn't do that to him. Would she? He glanced at Meg but she ducked her head.

That would explain Mac throwing daggers at him every time he looked his way. But Mac had been his usual self when he'd first arrived. So he must've seen something after he'd arrived. Something like father and daughter standing side by side.

And he couldn't blame Mac for being angry. Thinking that he'd abandoned the mother of his child, even if it was unintentional, filled him with burning shame.

Fiona drew his gaze again. He hadn't noticed it at first because her curly red hair had blinded him to her individual features. But those eyes and those dimples...

"So, about the roof. I—" Meg began.

"It's all sorted," her dad said, his tone cool.

"I'm going to buy the shingles and some of your dad's

firemen friends will put it on," he heard himself telling Meg and willed her to look at him.

Meg shook her head. "But I—"

Mac speared another pancake and plopped it on his plate. "You'll need to feed 'em and lay in a good supply of beer."

Meg stared at her plate. "Riley shouldn't have to pay for my roof."

"Maybe it's time the boy stepped up," Mac muttered.

Okay, here it comes. But no, Mac wouldn't say anything in front of Fiona. And neither would he, despite the growing need to demand answers.

Doris laid her hand on her husband's arm. "I was telling Meg that you and I would take Fiona down to the lake after breakfast. I want to see the princess tree."

Mac frowned at Doris. "A princess tree? What the—"

Meg interrupted, "Don't you remember when I was little, Dad? The poor tree was struck by lightning and grew all misshapen. I was so sad, you made up a story how it was waiting for the prince to come back to his princess."

Mac scowled. "That was ages ago. Don't tell me that gnarled old thing is still there."

"Yup and still standing." Meg glanced at Doris, but still refused to look him in the eye.

Fiona bounced in her seat. "It's still waiting for the prince, Grampa Mac."

Mac shook his head. "Well, I—"

Doris squeezed his arm. "Fiona wants to show it to me, don't you, sweetie?"

Fiona wiped her mouth. "I found it and Mommy told me how the king put it there to keep his princess safe while he was fighting the dragons. Are you coming, too, Mommy?"

I'm Fiona, like the princess. Her words came back and took on new meaning. His heart squeezed into his throat, choking him. Is that what Meg had told her to explain his absence in her life? Fairy tales instead of the truth? Instead of telling him so he could do the right thing?

Doris leaned over and hugged Fiona. "I think your mommy and Mr. Riley are going to clean up the dishes while we go."

Oh, yeah, they were going to clean up some things, but it sure as hell wouldn't be dishes.

Chapter Ten

Meg stacked the plates and brought them to the sink. Turning on the hot water, she held her hands under it, hoping to warm her chilled fingers. Her heart was beating so hard it hurt. Her mind whirled so fast she couldn't separate her thoughts. Oh, God, she needed more time. Yeah, as if that would make a difference.

He reached around her to shut the water off. "Does everyone on the planet know it but me?"

How dare he! She ground her teeth in anger and frustration. She crossed her arms to keep from reaching out and clocking him.

His eyes went hard and he stepped farther away from her. "Damn it all, Meghan, how could you?"

"How could I…?" She pressed a hand to her chest, leaving a wet palm print.

His nostrils flared. "You heard me. I expected better of you."

"You expected? What would you have preferred? That I didn't have her?" She choked on the last word.

"Of course not. I—"

"Or maybe I should've given her up. Would that have suited you and your life plans better?" The mere thought of life without Fiona shredded her and she choked back a sob. "My parents said they'd back me whatever decision I made and—"

"See? That's it right there." He leaned closer. "You talked it over with your parents and not me."

"They were there for me and you weren't. So you can take all that self-righteousness and moral superiority, Riley Cooper, and stuff it," she told him through gritted teeth. Her eyes burned and her vision blurred. "I did everything I could to contact you and all I got was silence. So don't you stand there now and blame this all on me. What the hell was I supposed to do?"

She uncrossed her arms and poked a finger in his chest. "I did everything I knew to get your attention. Your lack of response told me all I needed to know, and I had a child to think of. I had to focus on Fiona and not some guy who couldn't be bothered."

"You knew where I was." He took a step back. "What about the Red Cross? They could've—"

"Excuse me, but I was a little busy having a baby. Your baby, Riley Cooper, yours." She stepped closer and poked him again. "When and how was I supposed to gain your attention? Huh, can you tell me that?"

She swiped at her wet cheeks with the back of her hand. *Damn*. She hated crying in front of him, but the Band-Aid had been torn off and she was bleeding as if the wound was fresh. "What about all those letters I sent you?"

"I spent a lot of time in places without access and I—"

"And I was taking care of a newborn and a dying mother." She gave up trying to stop the tears, but she hated that they were even flowing. "And after she died my dad and brother looked to me as if I had the answers. Well, guess what? I didn't have a freakin' clue. So I gave up trying to reach you. I figured you couldn't care less whether you knew about it or not."

"Exactly how hard did you try?"

She planted her hands on her hips. "You may not have read any of those letters you returned, but you saw how many I sent. I mentioned my pregnancy in more than one. The last one said you had a daughter and I intended to do my best by her. Care to explain why you chose to return them instead of reading?"

"After I left, I realized you were still so young. You had college ahead of you and your dream of being a teacher. Hell, I didn't even know if I was going to make it back in one piece. I didn't want to rope you into a life-changing commitment before you—"

"Try having a child. I consider that the ultimate in lifetime commitments."

His eyes were as cold and hard as flint. "She's not some trophy you get to keep because you disapproved of my behavior."

He was right, but that fact fueled her anger. "Did you even bother to read any of them?"

He rubbed a hand over his face. "The first one. That was enough for me to know I couldn't put you through the hell my life might become. By the time I got that letter, I'd already seen enough to change me forever."

"So did I and I didn't even have to leave home to do it."

He flinched and she hoped her barbs had managed to hit an artery. Or two. She'd gladly stand here watching him bleed out and— Oh, who was she kidding? They needed to work together for Fiona's sake. What would happen to her baby if they couldn't come to terms with what they'd done?

She heaved a deep sigh. "The important thing now is Fiona. She didn't ask to be born to two screwed-up parents."

He flinched. "You don't need to lecture me about the parent lottery."

She brushed the fresh tears off her face. "What happens between us now is only important because it affects Fiona."

"I may have screwed up, but that doesn't compare with what you've done, Meghan." He covered his mouth with his hand, his fingers and thumb digging into his cheeks as if he were locking his words inside.

"I know that." Her anger was spent and in its place was a sadness that pressed down on her.

"I had every right to know... Do you have any idea how I feel when I think about all the things I've missed?" He dropped his hands to his sides ands blew out his breath. "You should've done everything in your power to tell me."

"I tried and you didn't care enough about me to open a letter."

He jerked back and tugged on his hair.

Regretting her harsh words even if he deserved them, she attempted to clear her clogged throat, failed, but managed to croak out, "You can get to know her now."

"Oh, you can bet on that."

She clasped her shaking hands together. He couldn't

take her baby away…could he? No, her dad and Liam wouldn't let that happen. *She* wouldn't let that happen.

"Has…" He swallowed. "Has she asked about me at all?"

"Only in the abstract, but I expected that to change once she starts school."

"Did…" He swallowed. "Did you tell her that story about the king fighting dragons for the princess?"

"I know it doesn't make up for my bad choices." She closed her eyes against the pain. "But I've made sure she had male role models in her life."

"Your dad and Liam?"

She nodded and wiped her face on her sleeve.

"Here." Riley held her chin in his hand and used the kitchen towel to wipe her face.

"Thanks," she whispered, but he shook his head.

He held up the towel. "Where do you want this?"

"Give it to me and I'll put it in the laundry." She grabbed the towel and set it aside, getting a fresh one from the drawer and setting it on the counter. "Thanks."

"For what? I haven't—"

Voices on the porch prevented them from saying anything more. Meg plastered a smile on her face as Fiona burst through the door, followed by Doris.

"Mommy, I saw a frog."

"You did?" Meg didn't dare look at Riley, but felt every inch of his presence as she wiped her hands on her jeans.

Fiona nodded, her pigtails bouncing like marionettes. "Uh-huh, but Mrs. Grampa Mac wouldn't let me kiss it to see if it was a prince."

"Thank goodness for Mrs. Grampa Mac. We don't

need any princes cluttering up the place." She straightened Fiona's glasses.

"But, Mommy…"

"But, Fiona…" Meg smoothed her flyaway hair and asked Doris, "Where's Dad?"

Doris glanced from her to Riley, who was staring at Fiona, his expression a mixture of longing and awe. "He's checking Matilda before we leave."

"Matilda?" Riley asked.

Fiona giggled. "That's what Grampa Mac calls his big camper. Isn't that funny? Don't you think so, Mr. Riley?"

"Yes, I do." Riley smiled at Fiona and nodded to Doris, but he held himself stiffly. "I'll go see if he needs any help."

Fiona started to follow. "I wanna help."

Doris called her back and said, "You promised me some of those cookies your mom made."

Meg mentally shook herself and prodded her daughter toward the kitchen. "Good idea. Milk and cookies. It's been practically an hour since we ate breakfast."

Doris laughed. "We did get some exercise."

Meg tried not to think about her dad and Riley in the yard, but that was impossible. She got out the cookies and milk and sat at the table with Fiona and Doris but didn't hear a word they said.

She jumped up and excused herself when the door opened. Her dad came inside alone but his face didn't look as grim as it had been when he'd left for the lake.

She wrung her hands. "Where's Riley?"

"Don't panic. I didn't finish him off. He was going over to his place. He said to tell you he'd be back over in a little bit."

She silently thanked Doris for keeping Fiona occupied, but she still kept her voice low. "So now you know the truth."

Mac stepped back onto the porch and she followed, pulling the door shut.

Mac glanced over to Riley's cottage. "He had the guts to face me. I have to give him points for that. He says he wants to make it right."

"What if he goes back to Afghanistan?" She and Fiona weren't enough for him. Riley was going back to his life as if nothing had changed.

Mac shrugged. "He's a marine. It's what he is, what he does."

She chewed on her lower lip. Clinging to her hurt and anger wasn't going to accomplish anything. "And I have to do what's best for Fiona."

Mac met her gaze. "Having a father would be good."

"Even an absent one?" Was she protecting Fiona or herself?

Her dad gave her an awkward hug. "I'm sure you'll do what's right for everyone. You always do. That's why I'm so proud of you."

She returned the hug, grateful for his support. "Thanks. That means a lot."

Riley paced the small kitchen, sipping a can of soda, trying to make sense of the lump of messy emotions pressing on his chest until he couldn't breathe. The irony of the situation was not lost on him as he paced around the kitchen. Had it only been a couple of weeks since he'd found Meg at the bottom of the stairs? He'd come here expecting to recover, not have his life implode.

And I didn't even have to leave home to do it.

Meg's words danced around his head as he paced.

Even his anger didn't prevent him from admiring all she'd accomplished as a single mother. She was giving Fiona the happy, stable childhood she'd experienced.

Damn. How could he be angry with her for taking such good care of his daughter? Because there was no doubt she was a happy, well-adjusted little girl.

He'd assured Mac he was willing to step up and do what was necessary to see that both Meg and Fiona were taken care of. How he would do that from Afghanistan was still a mystery. Her home needed a lot of repairs and upkeep. And what about Fiona? How could he make up for those missing years in the time he had left? He had five years to catch up on, and being responsible for a child meant more than sending child support checks. How was he supposed to get to know his daughter, let her get to know him, from halfway around the world?

At the thought of Meg and Fiona, his chest tightened and pressure began to build. What the hell did he know about being a father? Like he'd told Meg, it wasn't as if he'd had any role models. His own parents were a cautionary tale at best. He wouldn't have realized families could disagree without making their kids collateral damage if it hadn't been for the McBrides. And how did he repay them? By getting Meggie pregnant, then abandoning her. *Nice going, Cooper. You're lucky Mac didn't clean your clock out there.*

And Meg. She'd been in love with him her entire life and he'd repaid her by sleeping with her and leaving. He should've taken care of her, seen that she was okay after he'd shipped out. Marines pledged to leave no one behind in battle and yet he'd left Meg behind. Thinking he was doing the right thing was a lame excuse. Heck, Meg had thought she was doing the right thing.

He swore when he realized he'd squeezed the soda can so tight, its contents had overflowed.

Slamming the can on the counter, he rinsed his hands in the sink and grabbed a paper towel from the roll. He wiped his hands, the counter and the soda can before tossing the wadded paper into the trash.

He gulped what was left then crushed the can in his fist. *A kid*. He had a daughter. She was a whole person with wants, needs and likes that he knew nothing about. How much had he missed out on? He tried to imagine all the stuff that went along with having a child, like first words, first steps—all those firsts. He tossed the can toward the recycling bucket. It missed and landed on the floor. Christ, he didn't even know his own daughter's middle name or birthday. All that condemnation he'd thrown at his parents over the years and he was worse.

Would he have given up his time in the marines to stay with Meg and Fiona? Even now, he was planning to go back, craving the security the corps had given him. Did he know how to be in a normal relationship?

After the motor home left, he went back across the yard to Meg and Fiona. Standing on the porch, he rubbed his sweaty palms on his pants before knocking on the door.

He stepped inside and his gaze searched the family room for his daughter. "Where's Fiona? You didn't send her with your dad again?"

"No." She lifted her chin. "And I didn't send her the first time. They wanted to take her and she wanted to go."

He sighed. He hadn't meant it to sound like an accusation, but he was still trying to deal with the fact that he had a daughter he barely knew. He knew he was as much to blame as Meg, but logic didn't make the pain and anger go away. He felt as though Meg had betrayed him by keeping his daughter a secret.

"C'mon in and sit down. *She's* not going anywhere."

He folded his arms across his chest and stifled a groan at the pain the movements caused.

"Do you need anything? I think your pain meds are still in Liam's room. I'll go and—"

"I took something back at my place. I prefer a clear head." Christ, her concern made him feel like a heel. He'd accused her of being selfish, but in fact, he was the selfish one.

Meg gave him a beseeching look. "We don't have to do this yet. Maybe you two could get to know one another first…"

"And waste more time?" And didn't that make him sound like a first-class jerk. "Sorry, I didn't mean it the way it sounded."

Meg sighed. "Why don't you take a seat on the couch? I need to get my clothes out of the dryer before they become a wrinkled mess, then we'll talk to her."

Sit down before you fall over, Marine.

He sat and wiped the sweat off his forehead. What was wrong with him? He could leapfrog his men in an urban combat situation, but here he was panicking at facing a five-year-old.

Fiona wandered into the room with a tattered stuffed animal clutched in a choke hold. She beamed with enthusiasm when she spotted him. "You came back."

"Yes, I did." He sat up straighter. "Who is that you've got there?"

She held up the toy. "This is Mangy."

"Aptly named."

"Huh? My Grampa Mac named him. He calls him Fiona's Mangy Mutt, but he's also a Dalmatian. They ride on fire trucks. Did you know my Grampa Mac is a fireman? Mrs. Grampa Mac says Grampa Mac is…" She scrunched up her face. "She says he's re-re—"

"Retired?"

"Yeah, that's it. Are you re-retired like my Grampa Mac?"

"No, I'm a marine." Would she even know what a marine was? His chest tightened at the obvious hero worship in her voice when she mentioned Mac. *Hey, be glad she had a positive male role model in her life instead of whining*. He told his inner voice to shut the fudge up. *Yeah, like she can hear the thoughts in your head. Have you gone soft, Marine?* "Looks like you've had Mangy a long time."

She nodded enthusiastically. "I had him my whole life."

"You must love him." His voice sounded hoarse. That damn stuffed dog had been in her life longer than he had. He blinked and managed to keep a smile on his face. Not a good idea to scare her.

The pink wire-rimmed glasses lent a serious air to her cherubic face. "Uh-huh. Mangy helps when the scared comes and helps when you get boo-boos. He makes scary things not so scary."

Riley leaned forward and rested his forearms on his thighs. The thought of this little girl being frightened hollowed him out. His childhood had been full of scary moments and he didn't want that for her. But how could he protect her all the way from Afghanistan? How could he not return to his squad? He needed to honor Trejo's sacrifice. "And what things scare you, princess?"

"The tunder scares me."

The tightness on his chest eased. Weren't most kids afraid of thunder? "Loud noises like thunder can be pretty scary."

She pushed her glasses higher up her nose. "Mommy says it can't hurt me."

"Your mommy's right." God, he wanted to gather her close and tell her he'd never let anyone or anything hurt her, including himself.

"I know, but...but sometimes the scared just comes." She leaned toward him, her gray eyes large behind the lenses. "Does that ever happen to you, Mr. Riley?"

Before he could guard against them, memories from Afghanistan played like a video in his head. The pings from ammo rounds hitting metal, shouted contradictory commands, sand in his mouth and eyes, the unmistakable stench of death in his nose. He had to clear his throat—and his head—before he could answer. "Yes, sometimes scared just comes."

She smiled sweetly, reminding him so much of Meg that it hurt, and yet he realized she was her own person. A person he didn't know, and he wanted to hate Meg for that, but he was as much to blame, thinking he had all the answers and setting them on a course that brought them to this moment.

"Mr. Riley?" She put her hand on his knee. "If you ever need Mangy, you can use him."

"You're very generous." He had to force the words past his clogged throat. His heart felt as though it had cracked open. The first time he'd looked into Fiona's eyes—his gray eyes—his world had tilted. Now it was spinning.

Thinking he knew best, he'd made the fateful decision that had sent them down this path. And once again he was assuming he had all the answers.

Meg came back in and set a laundry basket on the arm of a chair. Her gaze met his and when he nodded, she said, "Sweetie, Mr. Riley and I have to tell you something important and very special."

"A surprise?" Fiona's eyes widened and she rocked on her tiptoes. "Am I getting my own swings with a slide and everything?"

Meg pulled on one of Fiona's pigtails. "Better than that."

Fiona came down flat on her feet. "My own doggie?"

Riley laughed at losing out to a swing set and a dog and the knotted tension in his chest eased.

"No dog yet, but I think you'll like this, too. Riley is—"

"A friend of your mom's," Riley interrupted. "And she wants us to become friends, too. Would you like that?"

"A grown-up friend?" she asked, her head tilted to the side to study him.

He didn't take his gaze off his daughter, but Meg's confusion was palpable. Yeah, he had some explaining to do, but this felt right. "We could do things together while I'm here and become friends."

"Can Mommy come, too?"

"Mommy is always welcome," he said and he meant it. He could spend his life blaming Meg, locked in a power struggle, but he wouldn't. He wouldn't become his father.

Chapter Eleven

After Fiona ran to her room, Riley was able to take a deep breath, his first since realizing the truth.

"I don't understand. Why did you do that?" Meg reached for a towel in the basket and folded it. "I thought you wanted to tell her."

"Faced with that trusting innocence, I couldn't do it." He sank back against the cushions. "I want her to know, but not until the time is right."

She set the towel on the arm of the chair. "Getting to know one another is a good first step. You're going to be her father for the rest of her life."

"And that reminds me of something that's been bothering me."

She picked up a little girl's nightgown and shook it out. "What is that?"

"How did it happen?"

"Happen?"

"We used a—" he lowered his voice and glanced down the hall toward Fiona's bedroom "—condom… each and every time."

Meg ran her fingers over the front of a pink nightgown. "True…"

"But?"

She blushed and looked away. "I guess there's a reason they caution to use them before the…uh, festivities begin."

"We…we— Oh." He shifted uncomfortably, remembering how eager he'd been that night, how both of them had been impatient, ripping one another's clothes off.

"Yeah, that time."

"I swear, Meggie, if I'd even suspected… I would have… I messed up." He drew his good hand over his face.

She smiled sadly. "That honor goes to both of us. I could have done more to track you down and tell you, but I let my pride and my anger get in the way."

"So what do we do now?" The time for anger, blame, hurt had passed. If his crappy childhood had taught him anything, it was that worrying about stuff that couldn't be changed was futile.

"You get to know her. You said you had the cottage for a month. Where will you go after that?"

"Afghanistan."

She grabbed on to the clothes basket. "So you're going back?"

"Of course. Why wouldn't I?" Had it only been last week that getting back had been his utmost priority?

"Why? I think that would be obvious."

"You mean because of Fiona?" He didn't tell her he'd

been having the same doubts. But he was a marine; the corps was his life. What would he do if not that? "I won't be the only one over there with a child back in the States."

"That's up to you. I guess that means you'll need to get to know your daughter while you're here."

"I'm planning on it." He would need to cram the short time he had left into getting to know Fiona and letting her get to know him.

Meg put the nightgown and towel back onto the pile of clothes. "You look exhausted. You still have some painkillers here. Want me to get them?"

"Ibuprofen is fine, if you have it." He tried to stand and winced, sitting back down. After finding out about Fiona, he'd been running on adrenaline. Now it was wearing off, and he felt every one of the bruises he'd suffered.

"Stay there. I'll get the pills," Meg told him.

"Meg, wait." He put a hand on her arm and winced when a look of uncertainty crossed over her beautiful features. He reached up and brushed off a curl that had stuck to her mouth. "Thank you for our beautiful daughter."

Several days later Meg sat on her porch enjoying a cup of coffee and watching Fiona on the new swing set Riley had bought. He'd said he wanted to make up for missing her other birthdays. If she'd let him, Meg was convinced their yard would be overrun with toys, but she didn't want Fiona to see him as a cash machine, or in this case, a toy machine.

The cedar set had a swing and a tree house–type structure at the top of a set of stairs with access to a slide and a sandbox underneath. It was way too elaborate but Riley insisted and she had to admit it was nice to see Fiona with something special.

A door slammed and Riley came out of his place and started across the yard.

"Mr. Riley." Fiona abandoned the swings and ran to take his hand. "Can you push me?"

Meg's eyes burned at the sight of the two of them. Seeing them like this, she knew she'd made the right decision. She hoped she felt the same after Riley left.

"I'll help you get going, then I need to talk to your mom."

After giving Fiona several pushes on the swing to get her going, Riley bounded up the steps onto the porch and sat next to Meg in the Adirondack chair that he'd insisted on replacing. "I ran into Jan at the Pic-N-Save."

Meg rolled her eyes. That damn grocery store was gossip central. "Oh, boy."

He stretched his long legs out in front and crossed them at the ankles. "Jan mentioned something about a bachelorette weekend. She said it was a pity you couldn't go because everyone has been looking forward to it."

"It's no big deal."

He tilted his head as he studied her. "If your reasons are financial, you know I will be paying child support from now on."

"And it's called child support for a reason. It's for her. Not me." She pulled her legs up and rested her cheek on her knees. "My reasons aren't monetary."

"When can we have a sleepover?" Fiona jumped onto the porch. "You said."

"We'll have to ask your mommy."

"Mommy?"

"You see Riley every day." The thought of having to share Fiona wasn't something she was quite ready to face. Her mind probed it like a tongue seeking a sore tooth, but pulled back at the first hint of pain.

"What about the bachelorette weekend with your friends?"

"What about it?" She turned to Fiona. "Sweetie, why don't you go play some more before it gets dark?"

He watched Fiona climb back onto the swings, and then turned to Meg. "I think you should go. I can stay here with Fiona."

"I don't know..." She nibbled on her lower lip.

"Don't you think I'm capable?" His eyes had grown distant.

She shook her head. "It's not that."

"Is it because of what happened at the church?"

"No, I trust you. Do you trust yourself?"

Riley squeezed his eyes shut as he bent over and gripped his knees. *Breathe, dammit.* One...two...three. The acid in his stomach churned and he swallowed several times before he straightened and called out, "Fiona...I'm not mad at you. Please come out."

Do you trust yourself?

Meg's words from three days ago came back to taunt him along with all his cocky reassurances that he could handle this. He was the one that had insisted Meg go away with her friends for the weekend. Taking care of Fiona on his own would help them bond. *Yeah, dumbass, you're doing just fine.*

He went to the front door for the umpteenth time and clenched the knob. Still locked and bolted. A quick glance at the clock before pouncing on the back door.

Still locked and bolted. *Sweet Jesus.* Four hours since they started that damn hide-and-seek game. He grabbed his phone with shaking hands. No more putting it off. Admitting defeat at his first test of parenting wasn't easy, but he had to face facts. And she was twenty minutes away at some sort of resort and spa. so she could return to her friends once they got this sorted.

He closed his eyes and pinched the bridge of his nose while waiting for the call to connect.

"Riley?"

"Meg, I—" He coughed hoping to disguise the shake in his voice.

"Riley? What is it? Is something wrong with Fiona?"

"Meg, I think you need to come home right away."

Chapter Twelve

Meg unlatched her seat belt and scrambled out as soon as Tina slowed the car.

Light spilled out of the open door of the cottage onto the porch and a police cruiser sat in the driveway next to Riley's truck.

Oh, God. Oh, God. Oh, God.

She tripped up the porch steps and rushed inside. Tina, who'd insisted on driving, followed up the steps. Riley, his shoulders slumped, his head bowed, stood deep in conversation with a uniformed officer.

"What happened? Where's Fiona?" Meg glanced around frantically. "Where's my baby?"

His red-rimmed eyes haunted, Riley took a hesitant step toward her. "We...we..." He drew in a shaky breath before continuing. "She wanted to play hide-and-seek. Each time she'd hide behind the couch or the bathroom door and giggle."

He drew a shaking hand over his gaunt face. "God, Meg, what have I done?"

Meg released the trapped air from her lungs and grabbed Riley's hand, pulling it away from his face, and started dragging him toward the master bedroom. "Quick. With me."

Please, God, let me be right. Without another word, she dragged Riley down the hall, the policeman and Tina trailing behind. Stopping in front of a giant wicker laundry basket inside the closet, she let go of Riley's hand and pulled the cover off.

"I'm not stupid. I already looked in there," Riley told her. "Nothing but clothes."

Meg leaned over and tossed the dirty clothes out, revealing Fiona curled up on the bottom, thumb in her mouth, Mangy tightly clasped to her chest, fast asleep.

"How the…?" Riley gasped.

"She did it to me once." Meg gave Riley a tearful smile. "Scared the heck out of me, too."

She reached in and put her hands under Fiona's arms so she could lift her out.

A sleepy Fiona blinked and smiled. "Mommy? You're home."

Meg pulled Fiona's thumb out of her mouth and hugged her as tightly as the child was clutching her toy. "Why did you scare Riley like that?"

"He scared me." Fiona rubbed her face on Meg's shoulder.

Out of the corner of her eye, Meg caught the police officer stiffening, but remained calm. "Why were you scared?"

"He said a bad word when I was hiding." Fiona's thumb crept toward her mouth and she narrowed her eyes at Riley. "You shouldn't say that. Mommy says it's bad. Really, really bad."

"I'll bet Riley was scared." Meg kissed Fiona's cheek. "People sometimes forget and say it when they're afraid."

Fiona scowled. "Why was he afraid?"

"Because—" Riley's Adam's apple bobbed "—I thought I'd lost you. I'm sorry I scared you, but I'm not used to playing games with girls."

Fiona toyed with the top button on Meg's blouse. "Why?"

"Because I spend most of my time with marines."

"Oh…well, I guess that's okay since this was your first time." Fiona held out her arms to Riley, and Meg handed her over.

Riley's eyes were moist as he held his daughter. The police officer cleared his throat and said, "Looks like everything is under control here."

Despite the bulky air cast, Riley clutched Fiona in one arm and stuck his free hand out to shake the cop's. "Thank you, sir."

The policeman shook his hand and gave him a curt nod. "Well, I'm glad it all worked out."

"I'm going, too," Tina whispered to Meg and followed the officer out.

Fiona tucked in her chin and touched Riley's face. "Are we still friends?"

"Yes, of course." He gave her a hug. "But next time, answer me when I call out for you."

She gave him a look full of exasperation. "But we was playing hide-go-seek."

Riley sighed and kissed the top of Fiona's head. "You got me there, kiddo."

* * *

After getting Fiona ready for bed, Meg tucked her in and gave her a kiss.

"Can Riley read me a story?" Fiona leaned to one side to look around Meg to Riley hovering in the doorway. "You promised."

Riley wiped his palms down the front of his jeans and glanced toward Meg, and her heart shrank. She hated that his first time alone with Fiona had been such a trial by fire.

"I'm sure he'd love to read to his favorite girl." Meg gave Fiona another kiss and went to the door, patting Riley on the arm as she left. "You look like you could use some coffee. I'll get it and we can talk when you're done."

Meg brought two mugs into the family room, setting one on the coffee table. She sipped hers while waiting.

"I screwed up tonight." He scrubbed his hands over his face and sank down next to her on the couch. "I'm so sorry I ruined your weekend. I had it all planned out in my head, just like our date. And the reality was that I stood by and watched it all go to hell and couldn't do a damn thing about it. Some father I turned out to be."

She couldn't help reaching out to touch his knee. "You have to do one thing and just one thing to be the best father in the world to her."

"And what's that?"

She pulled her hand away, embarrassed she'd reached out like that. "Love her. It's as simple as that. Can you do that?"

"Heck, I already do." He cleared his throat. "I will be making arrangements to take care of Fiona financially, but I want to take care of you, too, Meg."

Does he think you can't provide for your daughter? She swallowed hard and lifted her chin before saying, "Look, I agree, as a single mom I've had to prioritize a few things, but I think I've done pretty damn good. I own a home, have a job and Fiona will be going to a good school—"

He touched her arm. "That's not what I mean. This is coming out wrong."

"Define *this*?"

"I want us to be a family."

Just like when he suggested the date, she needed to know exactly what he meant. "Well…I'm her mother and you're her father, so I guess that means we are already."

"I want to make it official." He took her hands into his. "Marry me. We can get married before I go back to Afghanistan."

"I'm not in the mood for jokes right now." She pulled her hands away and fisted them until her nails dug into her palms. She'd waited years to hear Riley make a life-time commitment to her. And this is what she got? Why was anger her first reaction to something she'd longed for? *Because each time you dreamed of this day, Riley used the words* love, *not* duty *or* responsibility.

His brow pulled his face into an affronted frown. "This is no joke."

"Sounds like it to me. You go from sucking at hide-and-seek to proposing. Where's the logic in that?" She tried to laugh, but it died on her lips. Truth was, she wanted to be his wife, but damn him, he hadn't once mentioned love. Could she love him enough for the both of them? Would being in a lopsided relationship wear away on her? Could she give up everything she'd accomplished in Loon Lake to traipse after a man who hadn't said he loved her? The thought of being a military wife didn't bother her. The thought of being an unloved wife did.

"I was never so scared in all my life." He reached out and cupped her face in his palm. "We could be good together, Meggie."

Is that what she wanted? To be *good together*? She should back away from his touch so she could think clearly. She leaned toward him.

His Adam's apple bobbed when he swallowed. "I know you'd be giving up a lot for me, but I promise to work to be the best provider I can."

But she didn't want a provider. She could provide for herself. She wanted a partner, a lover, someone who couldn't bear to live without her. Was that too much to ask?

She could deal with uprooting every couple of years if she knew Riley loved her. She was proud of Riley and his service to his country, and if he wanted to stay in until retirement, she'd support him in every way possible. Heck, she'd be proud to hold down the home front and be there to welcome him home during deployments if Riley loved her. But he was treating marriage to her as his duty. Swallowing past the knot in her throat, she said, "I'm sorry, but I think we'd be making a mistake."

He frowned. "You think it would be a mistake to give Fiona a family?"

Yes, if one partner was miserable. "It may not always look like it, but we've made a good life for ourselves here."

"If you're worried about the military thing, I know we could make it work." He scratched his stubbly cheek.

If you loved me, I would make it work. The burn behind her eyes increased and she had trouble swallowing but she pushed on. "Getting married just for financial reasons doesn't make sense to me."

She waited, her hands clenched into fists, hoping he would dispute her words. Tell her he loved her and that was why he'd proposed. He didn't have to recite poetry, just use the word *love*.

"But it's my duty to take care of you and Fiona and I honor my obligations."

Hope faded away and her heart broke open as the word *duty* reverberated through her like an echo. "Your only duty to Fiona is to love her. You have no obligation to me whatsoever."

Riley stood at the window and stared across the yard at what he couldn't have, didn't deserve. He'd always known Meg was too good for the likes of him, but he'd begun to hope when she'd forgiven him for all he'd done. It was true he hadn't known about her pregnancy, but that fault was his and his alone. In the end, it didn't matter that he'd thought he'd been doing the right thing. He'd messed up and now he'd have to pay for it for the rest of his life unless he could figure out how to get Meg to change her mind. Three days and she hadn't budged, so hope was fading. He consoled himself with the fact that she had made sure whatever had happened between them, Meg went out of her way to cultivate his relationship with Fiona. There weren't many days left on his leave. At one time the original thirty days had stretched before him like an eternity; now it felt like incoming mortar rounds bearing down on him.

The bag of Jack bottles, still capped, mocked him from beside the front door. Yeah, getting drunk would impress Meg. Not to mention that would be a crap thing to do to Fiona.

His phone buzzed and he glanced at the picture a buddy had texted him and grinned. Stuffing the phone in his pocket, he went out the door and jogged across the yard.

Meg pulled the door open at his knock. "Hey."

"Hey," he said and paused as he drank in her warmth.

"Fiona's not back from the park yet." She nibbled on her bottom lip and Riley shifted, remembering how that sexy bottom lip tasted.

"I know." He pulled his phone out. "I wanted to run this by you first."

He turned the phone on and showed her the picture.

She grinned. "It's adorable. What is it?"

"I'm told it's an Australian and poodle mix, an Aussiedoodle puppy, but to me it looks like a canine version of Fiona, with those reddish curls and big eyes."

"You got that right." She laughed and handed him back the phone. "But why are you showing it to me?"

"A buddy of mine, his wife knows someone who breeds them or something, and he's offered this one to me for Fiona." He glanced at the puppy before shoving his phone back into his pocket. "He assures me it's hypoallergenic so you won't have to worry about your asthma and I'll take care of all the vet and food bills."

"How can I say no to that face?"

His or the puppy's? "Thanks. My buddy says he can meet me halfway between his house and here this afternoon. I can take Fiona if you'd like some time to yourself?"

Something in Meg's green eyes flickered, but all she said was, "That'd be great."

He nodded and started for home but turned back. "Uh, did you want to come?"

"No, I have things to do."

Riley couldn't tell who was more excited, Fiona or the puppy. She'd hugged him and chattered the whole drive back. At least he'd done something right. He'd only wished Meg had accompanied them.

He pulled into the driveway and scowled when he spotted an older model pickup. No wonder Meg hadn't wanted to tag along. She must've been expecting someone. He glanced in the rearview mirror but Fiona's attention was still on her new puppy, who leaned against her, his eyes closing.

"We're home." Fiona threw her skinny arms around the puppy, knocking her glasses askew. "This is where you live now, Mangy."

Riley sighed. "Are you sure you don't want to name him something else?"

"Nope." Fiona stuck her bottom lip out and shook her head fiercely. "He's Fiona's Mangy Mutt. You said I could keep him. You said."

"Okay…okay." Riley turned off the engine and saw the truck had Massachusetts plates. Did Meg have someone who still lived in—

"Uncle Leem," Fiona squealed and bounced in her booster seat. The puppy perked up and barked. "I can show him my new puppy."

Liam? What was Meg's brother doing here? His gut tightened. Had something happened to Meg while he was gone? He unbuckled his seat belt and jumped out of the truck, only stopping when Fiona began calling for him.

He turned on his heel and rushed back to the truck,

opened Fiona's door and helped her out of her seat. "Let me have Mangy's leash."

"But he's mine. You said."

Riley sucked in a deep breath. "I know that, but I need to help you down and I don't want him running off. He doesn't know his way around yet."

He managed to get both Fiona and the puppy out of the truck. Once on the ground, Fiona made a mad dash for the house, the puppy pulling on the leash and yipping in excitement, trying to follow the redheaded dynamo.

Riley and the dog caught up to Fiona as she burst through the door. "Mommy, we're home."

Meg came in from the kitchen. "I didn't think it was possible, but he's even cuter than his picture."

Liam came into the room and Fiona launched herself at him. "Uncle Leem, I got a puppy…a real live Mangy. And he's got hair like mine."

Liam picked up Fiona and turned her this way and that. "Hey, bug, you're right. He does have hair like you."

"Uncle Leem, it's me, Fiona." Fiona squirmed and giggled and pointed a finger at the dog. "That's my dog."

Liam drew his eyebrows together. "Are you sure?"

She giggled. "Uh-huh. Guess what else I got? A new friend."

Way to go, Cooper. Second billing to a dog. He glanced at Meg and she gave him a one-shoulder shrug.

Liam leaned down to set Fiona on the floor and she ran over to Riley and grabbed his hand. "See? He's my new grown-up friend. Mr. Riley."

Liam rose to his full height, an inch shorter than Riley, and faced him. He lowered his chin in acknowledgment. "Cooper."

"McBride." *Make nice and don't upset Fiona.* Riley

shifted his stance into parade rest. "I hope nothing's wrong."

"Nah. I started my off-duty rotation so I decided to come and visit my sister and favorite niece." Liam tugged on one of Fiona's pigtails. "Isn't that right, bug?"

"Hey." Fiona put her hands on her hips. "Mommy says I'm your only niece."

Liam made an exaggerated face. "I guess that's why you're my favorite. Hey, sis, I think your dog might need to go outside."

Indeed, the puppy was sniffing around. Fiona ran over and picked up his leash. "I wanna take Mangy outside."

Liam snorted. "Mangy? Were all the good names already taken?"

"Mommy," Fiona whined.

Meg shot her brother a deadly look. "Maybe Uncle Liam wants to take him out."

"I think Mommy and Fiona need to take him out," Liam shot back.

Meg narrowed her eyes. "Liam, this isn't any of your—"

"Meg, it's fine." Riley knew what Liam wanted. "I can—"

"Look, Mommy, Mangy is lifting his leg." Fiona pointed and Meg rushed to open the door, hustling Fiona and the puppy outside.

Liam slammed the door behind them, turning to Riley. "Why are you doing this to her?"

"What are you talking about?" Riley pulled his shoulders back. He understood brotherly concern, but he'd proposed to Meg and she'd refused him.

Liam took a step toward him. "She needs to get on with her life. How can she do that if you're hanging around?"

Riley didn't back down. No way was he giving up time to be with his daughter. "I'm Fiona's father. I have a right to be here."

"You have a right to be in Fiona's life, but you don't have to do that from next door."

"Maybe I want to be next door," Riley replied. Oh, yeah, and didn't that make him sound so mature.

Liam leaned closer. "Why? So you can break both their hearts when you leave?"

Chapter Thirteen

Riley shut his door and leaned against it, trying to regain control before he punched his fist through something. At least that pain would take his mind off the agony in his chest. It hurt to breathe. He was a marine, not some lovesick romantic fool.

She needs to get on with her life.

Is that what Meg wanted? To get on with her life without him?

How could he have been so wrong about Meg's feelings? Like some arrogant fool, he'd been convinced she'd jump at his proposal and he could install them in base housing, safe in the knowledge they'd be waiting for him between deployments.

Damn, he was a jackass. He'd wanted to take Meg away from the life she'd created, the home she loved, so she could follow behind him and be there for him while he breezed in and out of her life. He wasn't the husband Meg deserved.

He slid down the door and landed on his butt. Pulling his legs up and resting his arms on his knees, he hung his head. Oh, God, this hurt worse than when he'd woken up in the hospital after the blast that killed Trejo. At least then he knew those injuries would heal, but this…this would take more than time and rest. More than a simple bag of booze bottles.

He was going to have to let Meg go.

A week later, Riley parked his rental car on the street in front of a neatly tended, tan Craftsman-style bungalow in a Los Angeles suburb. His thoughts had kept coming back to one thing. He hated cutting his time with Meg and Fiona short, but he needed to lay the past to rest in order to go forward, so he'd driven to Boston and caught a flight to L.A. The image of Meg and Fiona waving from the porch of the cozy cottage shattered his heart like a mortar to the chest every time he thought about it. Even the puppy had looked forlorn.

He had two days left on his leave and then five until his appointment with his career counselor. If he signed those papers, he'd be obligated to the marines for another four years. A month ago it was a given he'd go back to Afghanistan and his men.

Now his shoulders slumped from the weight of the burden of this decision, but coming here was one way of closing the door on the past. He got out of the car and glanced around the blue-collar neighborhood, flexing his wrist now that it was free of the cast.

His gut churned as he strode up the cement walk. On the porch he tucked his cap under his arm, rang the bell and stood back. The glass storm door reflected his image back to him and he stared at the uniform he'd worn out of respect.

An attractive woman in her forties opened the inner door and he took another step back so she could open the outer door.

At first she frowned at him, her brown eyes wary. "Can I help you, Sergeant?"

She was familiar enough with the uniform to know his rank. "Ma'am, I'm sorry to intrude but I wanted to speak with you and your husband if he's home."

"Does this having anything to do with my...my son?"

"Yes, ma'am. I served with him in Afghanistan."

"Sergeant Cooper?"

He tried to swallow the lump in his throat and couldn't dislodge it, so he had to speak around it. "That's right, ma'am. I should have come sooner. I apologize for the delay."

She smiled. "I...well, I wasn't expecting you, so I guess you're not late, are you?"

"No, ma'am, not if you put it like that. Is your husband here?" He knew they'd be nice people before even meeting them. And yet, her gracious smile gutted him, but he had to do this not just for himself but for Meg and Fiona.

"Yes, he's here. Won't you come in? We just finished up lunch. Can I get you anything?" She stepped aside so he could enter.

"I don't want to intrude." And yet he was going to.

"Believe me, Sergeant, you're most welcome. If you don't want lunch, at least have coffee and cake with us. Alex told us so much about you in his letters and calls."

Riley swallowed hard. "He did?"

"Oh, yes, he spoke very highly of you. I think he thought of you as sort of a mentor."

He followed the woman through a tidy living room lined with photos of their son. A gold-framed picture of Trejo in his dress blues presided over the room from above the fireplace. His steps faltered as he stared at the young man who'd saved his sorry ass. *Trejo had spoken highly of me?* He'd never thought of himself as a mentor. He dragged his gaze away from the picture and followed the woman into a small but friendly kitchen with a round maple table and four chairs. The cheerful kitchen reminded him of Meg's and he blinked to clear his vision.

"Have a seat." The woman pointed to one of the chairs.

"Thanks, ma'am." He sat down but jumped up when a distinguished-looking man the same age as the woman came through a side door.

The older man's head jerked back when he spotted Riley.

"Ronald, this is Sergeant Cooper. The squad leader Alex spoke about."

The man came forward and thrust out his hand. After shaking hands, he pointed to the chair Riley had vacated. "Sit. Please. It's an honor to meet you, son."

Trejo's parents also took seats at the table.

Riley looked down at the cover clutched in his hand. "I'm not sure where to begin or even why I'm here but I…" He cleared his throat. "I wanted you to know that your son's actions saved my life that day. It was a selfless act of courage. I wanted to be sure you knew that. I know it's cold comfort, but I didn't know what else to do."

Trejo's mother placed her hand on his arm. "Thank

you. This means a lot to us. We've always been proud of Alex."

"As you should be, ma'am. Is there anything I can do for you? Anything you might need?"

"Do you have any children, Sergeant Cooper?"

Although confused by her question, he couldn't stop the automatic smile when he thought of Fiona. "Yes, I have a daughter. Her name is Fiona…like the princess."

The woman nodded. "I don't suppose you have a picture. I know everyone these days keeps all their pictures on their phones, but I still like good, old-fashioned paper ones."

"Yes, I do." Another strange question, but he pulled out his wallet. He had the picture of Meg and Fiona he'd swiped from Meg's refrigerator before leaving. He handed it over.

The woman smiled as she stared at the picture. "Your little girl is adorable. She looks like her mother, but I can see plenty of you in her, too. May I have this?"

"Of course." He was flummoxed but he couldn't say no.

"Thank you." She held up the picture. "When I think of Alex, I'll pull out this picture and know that because of my son, this sweet little girl will grow up with her daddy."

"I don't know what to say, ma'am." Riley had trouble getting the words past his thick throat, and though he blinked several times, his vision remained blurry.

"You've already said it, son, with that look on your face when you spoke about them." Ronald Trejo patted Riley's arm. "Love your family. That's good enough for us."

* * *

Riley's uniform had allowed him to catch an earlier flight back to Boston. He was exhausted after making the twelve-hour drive back to Camp Lejeune and should've felt relief as he passed through the front gates, but entering the base didn't feel like arriving home the way it had in the past.

You've already said it...with that look on your face when you spoke about them. Love your family. That's good enough for us.

Ronald Trejo's words played on a loop in his head. Why had he fought so hard to hide from the truth? Of course he loved Meg. He had for a long time, but had been too stubborn—no, make that scared—to admit it. He recalled the words he used when he proposed. He'd said words like *obligation* and *duty*. No wonder she refused him. She'd have to have been crazy to accept a proposal like that. Of course Meggie wanted love. She'd want a marriage based on love like her parents had, not one based on duty or anything else.

With a tired curse he dropped his pack on his bed in the bachelor quarters and unzipped it. He pushed the sides apart and froze. On top of the civilian clothes and skivvies sat a ragged, well-loved stuffed Dalmatian. *Holy hell.*

How had that gotten in there? Knowing how much Fiona doted on the stuffed critter, he could imagine the panic going on right now in the Loon Lake cottage. Poor Meg. She was probably trying to console Fiona while searching for the thing. He still couldn't imagine how he'd ended up with it.

Mangy helps when the scared comes and helps when you get boo-boos. Fiona's words came back to him. Meg must be his Mangy because she made his wounds hurt less; all the scars, emotional and physical, had hurt less when he'd made love to Meg. She couldn't undo or change the horrors he'd experienced, but she made the darkness they brought not so scary.

An envelope with his name written in Meg's neat, flowing cursive lay under the stuffed toy. He pulled it out and stared at it. The irony of the situation was not lost on him and his lip curled.

Knowing he'd hurt her and himself by returning her letters stole his breath. With shaking hands he opened the envelope and pulled out a legal document. Unfolding it, he saw it was a birth certificate. Fiona's birth certificate. His gaze went straight to *father*… There on the line was Riley James Cooper.

He stared at his name until the letters blurred together. When he was able to move, he unfolded the note.

I know this doesn't make up for the years you missed, but you've always been Fiona's father. Nothing will change that. And I love you. I always have and I always will. Nothing will change that, either.

He set the papers aside and picked up the stuffed Dalmatian. Holding Mangy, he could smell Fiona, Meg, the cottage, all of it, as if it were all trapped in the fake fur. Taking a deep breath, he let the weeks he'd spent in Loon Lake fill him.

"Oh, man, Coop's got himself a new friend." Another marine stood in the doorway.

Riley flipped him off. "It belongs to my daughter, you dumbass."

"Daughter? Didn't know you had any kids."

"Well, I do."

"How old is she?"

"Just turned five." Riley cleared his throat. "Her name's Fiona."

The guy shook his head. "What're you doin' back here? Why aren't you thanking your lucky stars you made it back in one piece?"

"My men need me," he said automatically, but his words lacked the conviction they'd once held.

"Not as much as they need to know it's possible to make it back so you can raise your kid." The guy's cell phone buzzed and he raised his hand. "Later, man."

Riley thought about what he'd said. Sure, he had an obligation to the men in his squad, but didn't he also have one to Meg and Fiona? He'd let Meg down in the past by abandoning her to face her pregnancy alone. It was true that he hadn't known about it, but now he did. This time, he had willfully abandoned her. How could he fault her if she turned to some other guy to share her life? If he lost her to someone else, the blame would be squarely on his shoulders. Even if he was leaving for as noble a cause as fighting for his country, the fact remained he'd left his family. He'd already served his obligation to the marines. Almost a decade's worth.

His finger shook and he had to swipe his screen a second time in order to call Meg.

"Riley?"

A large lump formed in his throat at the sound of her sweet, slightly husky voice, and he had to swallow twice before he could force any sound past it. "Hey, I… I wanted to let you know that somehow Mangy ended up in my gear."

"Good Lord," Meg muttered.

Still too raw, too hollowed out, he couldn't bring himself to mention the documents. Instead, he said, "Yeah, I figure things might have reached critical mass by now."

"She hasn't mentioned it. The fact that she now has a real-live puppy might have helped, although I'm not sure what will happen next time we have a thunderstorm. She's in her room—let me get her."

He heard noise in the background, followed by high-pitched chatter.

"Mr. Riley, you called me." Fiona sounded breathless.

His gut clenched. "I told you I would."

"Mommy didn't believe me."

He heard Meg protesting in the background. With his track record, he couldn't blame her. Meg said something about Mangy before Fiona came back on. "I don't have to give my real-live Mangy back, do I?"

He swallowed, trying to clear the clog in his throat. "No, he's all yours, but you have to help Mommy take care of him."

"I promise. Is that why you called me? To make sure I took good care of my new Mangy?"

"No, I called because somehow old Mangy got into my duffel bag and came to the base with me."

"Does he like it there? I told him he needed to take care of you when the scared comes."

"You put him in my bag on purpose?"

"Uh-huh. I was worried about what you would do when the scared came. And I didn't want you to forget me or Mommy."

"I… I…" He cleared his throat. "I could never forget my girls… I… I need to go now, princess."

"Okay, we love you…"

"I love you, too." He could barely see his screen to end the call.

Riley was thankful he was alone. Christ, if anyone saw him now, they'd take his man card and run it through a shredder. A grown-ass marine bawling like a baby.

After Riley's phone call, Meg and Fiona sat down to a quiet supper.

"Why did you send Mangy with Mr. Riley?" Meg was still trying to get over the fact that Fiona had let her precious stuffed animal go.

"I saw you put something into his bag and I wanted to give him something of mine because I knew how sad he was." Fiona picked at her supper. "When we went to the lake and I showed him my princess tree, he told me all about the king who had to go away."

Meg pushed her green beans across the plate. "He did?"

"Uh-huh. He told me how much it hurt the king to leave the queen and the little princess but he had to fight the dragons." Fiona stabbed a bean and stuck it in her mouth and frowned.

"That's a story, sweetie. Like the princess movies you like to watch."

Fiona dropped her fork with a clatter and stuck out her chin. "Mr. Riley said I was the princess in the story."

Meg pushed her plate aside. "Yes, sweetie, but it was a story he made up. He was being nice when you showed him your tree."

"Doesn't he like me?"

Just because he's nice doesn't mean he likes you. Oh, God, what was she doing? Meg's arms curled around her stomach, remembering how those words hurt. Liam probably didn't even remember them and here she was dragging them around with her like a battered suitcase.

What kind of mother was she, doing that to her own daughter? She choked back a sob.

"Mommy?" Fiona slipped off her chair and went to Meg.

Meg pulled her onto her lap. "Oh, sweetie, Riley loves you more than anything in the world. I know he'd be here with us if he could. And he was very sad to leave us."

Fiona put her arms around Meg and buried her face in her neck. "I misses him."

Meg rocked her. "So do I."

The puppy came over and whined, trying to wedge his face between their bodies. Meg couldn't help but laugh because he was so freaking cute. Fiona ended up giggling, too.

"How about we take Mangy for a walk to the lake to check on your tree?"

"Can we, Mommy?"

"Sure."

The puppy yipped in agreement and began dancing around.

"And when we come back, you can draw some pictures and we'll send them to Riley as soon as we get his address."

"Can we send him pictures every day?"

"I think that's a very good idea." Meg realized she meant it. She didn't want to discourage Fiona and Riley's relationship. She wanted Fiona to believe in fairy tales and happy endings. They might not always happen for everyone, but to take away her beliefs would be sad. "Let's put Mangy's leash on him and go to the lake."

"Can I hold his leash, Mommy?"

"Be sure to hold it tight."

The excited puppy dragged them to the lake.

"Mommy, look!" Fiona pointed to her princess tree. "He's coming home. Isn't that good?"

"Well, I…" Meg couldn't believe what she saw. The tree had fallen. She vacillated between letting Fiona keep her dreams and letting her know that Riley might not be coming back…ever. No—she pushed that thought aside. Even if she didn't believe in fairy tales for herself, the thought something could happen to Riley in Afghanistan was something even she refused to believe.

"When's he comin' home?"

A smile was beyond her, but Meg hoped she didn't sound as fatalistic as she felt when she said, "I guess we'll have to wait and see, sweetie."

She clung to hope like a life preserver, afraid if she lost it, she'd drown in a sea of despair. Riley had taken a picture off the refrigerator before he left. The one of her and Fiona together. Why that one? Why not one of Fiona alone? That had to mean something. He'd shown how much he cared in a dozen little ways, even if he hadn't said the words she longed to hear.

Chapter Fourteen

The excited puppy chased after a meandering butterfly, lunging into the air and falling flat on his tummy. Meg smiled at his antics, unable to resist his zest for life, but her heart still ached and every night she cried herself to sleep out of sight of Fiona. Meg did her best to put up a good front for her daughter, but she knew it would take a long time, if ever, for her to get over Riley. She wished she had Fiona's unwavering conviction that Riley would be returning to them soon. It had been only ten days since he'd left, but it felt like a lifetime. How could she have grown so accustomed to his presence in such a short time?

She pulled her feet onto the Adirondack chair and rested her chin on her knees. The curly-haired puppy ran onto the porch and lapped up water from the dish beside Meg's chair. With a tired sigh, he flopped down.

He was a canine version of Fiona, with his coppery curls and boundless energy. The poor thing was stuck with the name Mangy, but that was what you got when you let a five-year-old name a dog. Meg's tired sigh matched the dog's.

Even with the rambunctious puppy to keep her entertained, Meg's thoughts strayed to Riley. Was he on his way back to Afghanistan? He'd called every night to talk to Fiona, but he'd missed the past three nights. Each time she'd tried to find out his plans, he changed the subject and pride prevented her from begging for information. Would the next time she heard from him be from some marine base in that or some other war-torn country?

Mangy's head popped up and he whined. A car pulled into the driveway and Meg dropped her feet to the floor. Rising slowly, she stared at her old rattletrap of a car. Riley had retrieved it from Ogle's garage and insisted on leaving his truck for her. She had argued but lost when he said he wanted Fiona to be safe and not stranded on the roadside somewhere. The puppy scrambled to his feet and she grabbed his collar, tamping down the hope that was trying to claw its way into her heart.

The car rolled to a stop behind Riley's truck. The dog barked and wagged his tail as Riley emerged from the driver's side and approached the porch. He stood for a moment and stared at Meg. The dog whined and lifted his head as if to ask his mistress if the stranger was friend or foe.

"Beats me," she whispered to the dog.

She tried to think of something to say, but all of the things she'd planned flew right out of her head. She felt sixteen, all awkward and tongue-tied.

Riley removed his sunglasses and slipped them onto

the neck of his T-shirt. He rested a foot on the first step and glanced from the dog to her. "You're not going to sic your dog on me, are you?"

"Depends on why you're here." The dog whined and yanked on her arm.

"Where's Fiona?"

"Vacation bible school at the Methodist church." She swallowed and rubbed the dog's silky fur. "You haven't told me why you're here."

"To tell you what an idiot I am, but you already know that."

"Let me put him inside. I'd like to hear more about this idiot business." Her hands shook as she tried to get the door open. After shooing the dog back inside and shutting the door, she turned back to Riley, her arms folded across her chest. "Fiona missed your calls the last few nights."

He raised an eyebrow. "Only Fiona?"

She shrugged nonchalantly, but inside she was quaking. "Why didn't you call?"

"Several reasons." He stepped onto the porch. "For one, I went to see Alex Trejo's parents."

She blinked. "The marine who saved your life? What happened?"

He shook his head, still in awe over what had happened. "They want to meet you and Fiona."

Meg jerked her head back. "They do? Why? How did they even know about us?"

"I told them." This time he shrugged, but the look in his stormy eyes told her this was anything but casual. "I'll always feel bad over what happened, but his mother made me see I would be disrespecting what her son did if I wasted my second chance at life because of guilt."

"She sounds like a smart woman."

"I need to show you something." He pulled his wallet out of his back pocket. He flipped it open and pulled out a small piece of folded paper.

"What is that?" She eyed the piece of battered composition paper. Could that be...?

"I want you to see this." He opened the paper and smoothed it out across his chest before handing it to her.

Her mouth dropped open. "It's...it's my first letter to you."

He moved closer to her and inhaled deeply.

She kept looking from him to the letter. "You kept it? I... I don't know what to say. It looks like...like...like it's been through a war."

"It has, and as you can see, I read it over and over." Color rose on his cheeks.

"But I don't understand. You acted like...like..." Her voice caught on the last word.

He stepped closer. "Aww, Meggie, I'm so sorry. You, through this letter, kept me company the whole time I was over there. Some nights...when things got bad, I read it more than once. I had it with me in the hospital, too."

She brought her hand to her mouth as she read her words from six years ago. "It was childish. Oh, God, I can't believe I wrote stuff like this to you."

He reached over and took her hand away from her mouth and brought it to his. He kissed her fingers. "It may seem childish, but I swear I cherished it. As you can see, I carried it with me the whole time I was over there. It was my good luck charm and...and my reason for making it through the tough times."

"But why did you return all the others without even opening them? I still don't understand."

"I know you don't and I'm sorry." He squeezed her hand between both of his. "I can't begin to explain how I felt. Instead of hating me for seducing you and taking your virginity, you—"

"You didn't seduce me. I seduced you and I would do it all over again, even knowing what I know now."

"We can discuss that later, but for now I want to explain." He cleared his throat and kept his grip on her hand. "Our Humvee was in a mortar attack and we sustained heavy damage… One of the guys bled out on what was supposed to be his last mission. He was going home."

He rubbed his palm on his thigh. "When we got back to base, word was waiting for him that his wife had gone into early labor and he had a healthy baby boy."

Her gaze met his. "I can't begin to imagine what it must've been like for you and—"

He put his fingers over her mouth. "Please. Let me finish my explanation before I lose my nerve. I… I need you to understand about everything. All of it. Those words you wrote…the feelings behind them…well, to be honest, they scared me. I was afraid to hope. I thought for sure you'd grow up, come to your senses and realize you could do better. And if I let you get any closer, you would have destroyed me. So I pushed you away. I pushed you away so hard and so cruelly, I knew I didn't stand a second chance with you…even when it was— and still is—my greatest wish."

"Maybe if you proposed again, I'd accept." She poked his shoulder. "I admit I love it here, but I love you more,

Riley Cooper, and I just want to be with you...wherever and however I can."

"I may be crap at showing it, but I love you. I have always loved you...even when you were a pesky kid with braces." He cupped her face in his hands and smiled when she didn't pull away. "Then I fell madly, deeply, hopelessly in love with the woman you became. I've never been able to make all the pieces inside me fit together without you. Being with you makes all the puzzle pieces fit."

He caught her tears with his thumbs. "Please don't cry, Meggie. I don't want to make you cry ever again."

"Then don't," she choked out. "Just...just love me."

"I love you, Meggie McBride." He gulped in air. "I have my marine discharge papers and I'm ready to move on."

"Discharge? But you love the marines. I would never take that away from you. My refusal of your proposal had nothing to do with you being a marine, but everything to do with what was missing in your proposal."

"You mean the fact that I love you and can't stand the thought of living without you?"

"Yeah, that. I—"

He cut her off with a kiss. When he pulled away, he rested his forehead against hers. "I spoke with Jeff and—"

"Who's Jeff?"

"The cop that came the night I lost Fiona. He's an Afghanistan vet, too. He said a couple of the guys are reaching retirement age and they'll be looking to hire soon."

"Here in Loon Lake?"

"Yup and I've enrolled in the next training academy course." His gray eyes flickered with uncertainty. "If that's okay with you."

"I love you no matter what you decide to do. You don't have to do this for me. You can stay in the marines. I know how much you love it."

A car pulled into the driveway before he could respond.

"Fiona's home," Meg said, taking a step back.

"Perfect timing." He squeezed her hand.

Meg glanced at him but the happiness shining in his eyes told her his words were sincere with no hint of sarcasm.

Meg left him to help Fiona, who'd spotted Riley and was bouncing up and down in her seat, eager to get out of the car. She opened the rear door and greeted her friend Tina and her two kids.

"Mommy, look. Mr. Riley's back," Fiona cried out.

"I see that." Meg retrieved the booster seat Fiona had abandoned and smiled at Tina. "I'll call you later?"

Tina glanced at Riley and laughed. "I'm guessing much, much later."

"Tomorrow?" Meg grinned, feeling giddy.

Tina waved her off and Meg followed Fiona to the porch at a more sedate pace.

Fiona squealed and launched herself at Riley, who was hunkering down with his arms outstretched. He caught Fiona and twirled her around.

"Now that's what I call a homecoming," Riley said and set Fiona down.

"Are you gonna stay with us some more?" Fiona jumped up and down.

"As a matter of fact, I was just getting to that part." Riley tugged on a pigtail.

"Huh? What part?" Fiona scrunched her nose.

Meg laughed, but she was thinking the same thing.

"I need both of you to sit. Fiona, you can sit on your mom's lap."

Fiona looked up at Meg. "Mommy?"

"Let's do as he says and we'll find out," Meg suggested and sat in the Adirondack chair. Fiona scrambled onto her lap.

Once they were seated, Riley got down on one knee in front of them.

"Mommy, what's he doing?"

"I'm asking you and your mommy to marry me." His gaze met Meg's, love shining in his gray eyes.

"Say yes, Mommy." Fiona patted Meg's cheek. "Say yes, *puh-leeze*."

He fished into his pants pocket and held out his hand. Meg gasped at the diamond band nestled in his palm.

"Will you marry me, Meghan McBride?"

"Yes, a thousand times, yes," she whispered and he slid the ring on her finger.

"Do I get a ring, too?" Fiona asked.

"Fiona," Meg chastised. Seeing the look of panic on Riley's face, she hurried to reassure him. "It's really not—"

"How about…" He unbuttoned the front pocket of his desert fatigues and pulled out a cigar. "When I accepted this, I had no clue this would come in handy."

What was he doing? You couldn't give… She drew a

deep breath. Riley was going to be a great dad, but she was going to have to trust him to do things his way. He slipped the paper band off the cigar.

"Hold out your hand, princess," he said and slipped the paper ring onto Fiona's finger. "I promise to be your daddy for the rest of my life and to love you forever."

"My daddy?" Fiona's eyes widened. "You're gonna be my very own daddy?"

"I may not have always been here with you and Mommy, but you, Fiona, have been my daughter from the day you were born and you always will be, no matter what. Now—" He cleared his throat. "Now I'm hoping you'll let me stay here with you and Mommy so I can be your daddy for the rest of your life."

"You'll live with us forever and ever and you won't go away no more to fight dragons?"

"Forever and ever. I promise." His gaze shifted to Meg. "I'm home to stay. I've slain all my dragons."

Riley and Fiona's voices drifted into the kitchen from the family room and Meg smiled. She'd finished cleaning up after supper, but it had taken her twice as long because she kept stopping to admire her diamond engagement ring. Riley loved her.

"I had planned on helping. You didn't have to miss the end of the movie," Riley said from the doorway.

She grinned. "It's okay. I've seen it a few million times already."

"Well, you'll be relieved to know E.T. is safely on his way home." He sauntered in and came up behind to pull her close, nuzzling her neck.

"Thank goodness. I worry about that every time,"

she said and angled her head to give him better access. "Because I want everyone—even a three-foot alien—to be as happy as I am right now."

"Mmm." He kissed the spot where her neck and shoulder met. "If he has something as wonderful as this waiting for him at home, believe me, he'll be the second-happiest guy in the universe."

"Second?"

He kissed his way across her jaw. "He has to get in line behind me."

It was a good thing Riley's arms anchored her to the floor, otherwise she'd be floating on the ceiling. "Where's Fiona?"

"She's picking out a book for me to read before bed."

"Are you gonna be okay with giving up the marines for watching kids' movies and reading bedtime stories?"

"Absolutely." He kissed his way back to her neck and pulled her earlobe into his mouth and nipped. "There's only one thing that could make this any better."

She was having trouble concentrating. "Wha-what would that be?"

"How about a half dozen more redheaded little girls calling me Daddy?" he asked, his gray eyes glinting.

"Six?" she squeaked.

He grinned. "Okay, maybe two or three."

"I'll think about it, but I told you before, Riley Cooper, that my hair's not red, it's—*mmmhhff.*"

He cut her off with a kiss.

"Was that a yes to two or three more?" he asked and pulled away to study her face.

She grabbed his shirt, tugging him closer. "Mmm…

I guess we'll need to start working on that part and see what happens."

"Daddy, I picked out my story," Fiona called from the other room.

He sighed. "Duty calls."

Meg gave him one last kiss. "Read fast."

* * * * *

MILLS & BOON

Coming next month

BABY SURPRISE FOR THE
SPANISH BILLIONAIRE
Jessica Gilmore

'Don't you think it's fun to be just a little spontaneous every now and then?' Leo continued, his voice still low, still mesmerising.

No, Anna's mind said firmly, but her mouth didn't get the memo. 'What do you have in mind?'

His mouth curved triumphantly and Anna's breath caught, her mind running with infinite possibilities, her pulse hammering, so loud she could hardly hear him for the rush of blood in her ears.

'Nothing too scary,' he said, his words far more reassuring than his tone. 'What do you say to a well-earned and unscheduled break?'

'We're having a break.'

'A proper break. Let's take out the *La Reina Pirata*—' his voice caressed his boat's name lovingly '—and see where we end up. An afternoon, an evening, out on the waves. What do you say?'

Anna reached for her notebook, as if it were a shield against his siren's song. 'There's too much to do . . .'

'I'm ahead of schedule.'

'We can't just head out with no destination!'

'This coastline is perfectly safe if you know what

you're doing.' He grinned wolfishly. 'I know exactly what I'm doing.'

Anna's stomach lurched even as her whole body tingled. She didn't doubt it. 'I . . .' She couldn't, she shouldn't, she had responsibilities, remember? Lists, more lists, and spreadsheets and budgets, all needing attention.

But Rosa would. Without a backwards glance. She wouldn't even bring a toothbrush.

Remember what happened last time you decided to act like Rosa, her conscience admonished her, but Anna didn't want to remember. Besides, this was different. She wasn't trying to impress anyone; she wasn't ridiculously besotted, she was just an overworked, overtired young woman who wanted to feel, to be, her age for a short while.

'Okay, then,' she said, rising to her feet, enjoying the surprise flaring in Leo di Marquez's far too dark, far too melting eyes. 'Let's go.'

Continue reading
BABY SURPRISE FOR THE
SPANISH BILLIONAIRE
Jessica Gilmore

Available next month
www.millsandboon.co.uk

LET'S TALK
Romance

For exclusive extracts, competitions
and special offers, find us online:

  f facebook.com/millsandboon

  ⬡ @millsandboonuk

  🐦 @millsandboon

Or get in touch on 0844 844 1351*

For all the latest titles coming soon, visit
millsandboon.co.uk/nextmonth